Ride the White Tiger

With Illustrations by Kim

RIDE THE WHITE TIGER

BY ROGER W. CLARK

Little, Brown and Company

Boston   L B   Toronto

*Published simultaneously in Canada
by Little, Brown & Company (Canada) Limited*

PRINTED IN THE UNITED STATES OF AMERICA

This book is dedicated to

KIM

who dared to ride the white tiger

Contents

Ride the White Tiger

I Enter the Enemy

IT HAD all happened so fast. Lee looked quickly through his
father's desk to see if he had forgotten anything. There was so
little time, but he would need anything of value, anything
that they might be able to sell later.

"I am ready." His mother, her face gray with fear, spoke
from the doorway. Lee straightened. "I can find nothing here."
Then his eyes saw the little jade paperweight in one corner
of the drawer. He picked it up, feeling the eternally cold stone
smooth in his hand.

"Are you sure that you have everything?" He did not look around, but kept his eyes in front of him, hidden by the deep shadows. Just a moment, that was all he needed. He didn't want Choo to see the tears that glimmered in his eyes.

She understood and said, "I will look again in the kitchen to see if there is something not remembered."

After she had left the doorway, Lee picked up the wavering candle and, holding it high, looked around the room. This had been his father's workroom. The huge mahogany desk with its many scratches, the tilted office chair, the large framed photograph of Seoul as seen from the top of the hill in Nam San Park — all of these things were his father's. They represented a peaceful and industrious life, a life that was collapsing with a dull booming sound that grew more and more clear through the rain-washed night.

Lee went to the sliding panel that led to the garden. Opening it, he felt the cool, moist air rush against his face. The guttering candle went out. Somewhere in the night an enemy was advancing on the city. The sound of heavy guns came muted through the rain, as softly cadenced as a funeral march. Somewhere in the darkness, Mr. Lee was working to burn records that might help the enemy when the city fell. Lee remembered his father's words just before he had left to join the other men. "You are the man of the house, now. You must take my place." A door closing, a sound of hurried foot-steps, and Lee was alone.

He straightened, and turned back to the room, sliding the door shut against the memory.

"Mother," he called down the dark hall. The kitchen door opened, and candlelight framed his mother's figure as she stood there waiting for him. Her hands nervously smoothed the full white skirt that reached to her ankles, and then the hands moved up to adjust the silver hairpin that kept the big glossy bun of hair in place low on her neck. From behind her skirts Lee's younger brother, Yung Sin, stared with eyes wide with fear.

"I have locked all the doors. If anyone tries to enter in our absence, he will have a difficult time," Choo said as she pushed Yung Sin before her. "I will put the keys in a familiar place so Father can find them if he should come back here before leaving the city."

They went out into the rain that had turned their alley into a mudhole. Choo carefully locked the door, and then hid the key on a concealed nail. Staying close together, they splashed up the alley toward the street.

The muffled sound of many voices swirled about them as Lee pushed his way into the swarming mass of refugees that jammed the street. The sounds of gunfire came a little louder through the rain from the north. Lee tried to swallow the blind panic that churned within him, a fear that was in the tide of people moving inch by inch through the gloom. Frequent crashes of thunder drowned out all sound, and the blue-white lightning made the rain-drenched mob cringe.

In minutes Lee was soaking wet. He kept darting looks over his shoulder to check on the other two. It would be too easy to become separated in the crowd. Choo was behind Yung Sin, her hand twisted tightly in his jacket. Terror was etched across her face. Her bulky dress was heavy with water, and clung to her. Lee did not try to speak. He needed all of his energy to force a way through the roaring crowd. There must be all of Seoul here, he thought. Thousands of people with one thought, escape. Lee realized that they were thinking as he was, that they must get to the Han River bridge before Seoul fell.

Escape. The thought was burning in Lee's mind. He led on, pushing, edging through wherever a space opened. Step by step they inched their way south toward the bridge.

Some of the fearful words running through the people near him penetrated his mind. He knew that there was only a grain of truth in a bushel of rumors, and he tried to find that grain.

"The Communists are going to destroy Seoul . . . turn it to dust . . ."

"They will kill all who stay . . ."

". . . soldiers said that the army would blow up the bridge as soon as all the troops have retreated across it."

He held onto that last comment, looking at his watch. Nine-thirty. The army couldn't cross the bridge with all of its equipment before dawn. But, he thought, the army is running away. The soldiers were probably as frightened as these people seeking escape. Frightened men were unpredictable. It would take at least three hours to get to the bridge. They should have time. Lee tried to push faster, but the human wall was impenetrable. Forcing impatience out of his mind, he just kept blindly moving with the people. Lee looked again over his shoulder, reaching back to touch his brother.

"Are you all right, Mother?" He shouted the words as loudly as he could. In the flashing lightning he saw her nod, understanding, and then she motioned him to go on.

The voices rose louder, drowning out the gunfire completely as they approached the river. Straining to see above the many heads, Lee could make out the steel skeleton hump of the bridge rising high in the night. Headlights of army trucks glimmered dimly through the rain, and the scene flared into sharp relief when a sheet of lightning crackled across the jet sky. He could see, too, the great hordes of people all trying to force their way over the bridge. It was twelve-thirty. Despair clutched at him. It would take many hours to cross here, and there was no other way out. Grabbing his brother's hand, he rammed his way diagonally through the people, shoving his way out to an almost deserted side street. He drew his mother and Yung Sin into the shelter of a shop doorway, and leaned back to catch his breath.

"Why are we stopping?" Choo gasped, wiping the rain from her face.

"We must hurry or it will be too late," Yung Sin cried fearfully. Lee tried to see the two faces in the darkness, but they were formless gray shadows before him. He said, "I do not think that we can go on. The people are moving so slowly that we may still be on the bridge when the soldiers blow it up. I think that it is wiser not to cross."

"But the Communists are almost here!" Choo cried, fear making her voice shrill. "They will seek us out and we will all be killed. We cannot afford to stay." She wrung her hands as she spoke, trying to make Lee see the urgency of their plight. He knew that they would be taking a terrible chance if they did stay. Many tales had come down from

North Korea describing the horrors of which the Communists were capable.

"What do you think, Yung Sin?" But even before his
brother spoke in his excited voice, Lee knew that he would
agree with Mother. He listened for a moment, then said,
"Come, we will go down to the river and see what is happening there. Then we will decide." They followed him back
into the slashing rain, and clung to his jacket tightly as he
forced his way back into the human river.

Lee stared at the unbelievable jam on the bridge. People
on both sides were being pushed into the water from the
pressure of the moving crowd. Screams of the drowning
rose thinly above the mob's roar. On one bank, a rowboat
was trying vainly to ferry some of the refugees across. Too
many people crowded into the boat. When the skiff reached
the strong midstream current, it overturned, throwing the
passengers into the swift black water. Most of the people
could not swim. Their heads bobbed for a moment, then
their heavy clothes pulled them under. Those who could
swim pushed the boat back to shore. It was turned right side
up, and promptly overloaded again by the frightened people.

Lee found a slight shelter behind an overturned army
truck which had been deserted, its headlights still burning.

They huddled together, their teeth chattering with the damp cold. He watched the swarming hordes of people trying to fight their way onto the bridge. The last of the army trucks, horns blaring steadily, pushed their way through the center. As Lee watched, a jagged bolt of lightning stabbed through the rain. It hit a telephone pole on the bridge with a blinding blue flash, and he staggered back covering his eyes. A wild cry tore from thousands of throats, "Bombs . . . bombs!!" Panic seized the people. Men and women began leaping from the bridge railings in blind fear. Their white-clothed bodies gleamed for a second, their screams echoed for a moment, and then the black waters swept them away.

Choo pulled Lee down against the truck, clinging to him. Yung Sin was crying, burrowing his face into Choo's skirts.

Suddenly an ear-splitting blast drowned out all else, tearing the tortured night. Another, and another as great red flames leaped hungrily into the wet sky. Choo whimpered against her son as chunks of cement and steel rained about them.

It had happened. The frightened soldiers were blowing up the bridge. Somewhere a panic-shaken hand was pressing hundreds of people into terrible death. A wailing cry went up from the thousands cowering on the beaches, an anguish-born moan as the people saw escape crumble before them crashing into the river . . .

Lee loosened himself from his mother's grasp, and stood up slowly. The dancing flames flickered across the twisted skeleton of the destroyed bridge. He reached down and firmly lifted Choo to her feet. "Come. We will go to Aunt's house. It is not very far. We should be safe there." Choo and Yung Sin followed Lee as he turned and walked down the river bank away from the wild sounds behind.

When they reached the aunt's house, she took them in without any delay. Her bustling little figure hurried them into the warm kitchen where she stoked up the fire. Moving with unaccustomed rapidity, she darted into the bedroom gathering blankets and dry clothes. As she moved, she kept shouting questions at them until she had the whole story.

"And where is my brother now?" she asked, hoisting a small iron pot of water onto the low stove.

"He went to the district office with some other men. They were going to destroy the records which showed who was against the Communists in Seoul. From there they were going to Pahk's house for the rest of the night." Choo spoke rapidly as she slipped behind a screen and began removing her wet things.

"Here," Aunt said, throwing a dress over the top of the

screen. "Wear this. It is not high fashion, but it will give your clothes a chance to dry. Now, tell me how my brother is going to get out of the city." Aunt clucked at the pot, which had not yet started to boil. She stooped to draw an earthen jug of rice wine out of a low cupboard near the stove. Setting this near the fire to warm, she listened to Choo.

"They have a boat hidden down the river to cross with. Then they plan to go into the hills working their way south at night, resting in the day." Choo's voice was muffled as she pulled on the dress.

"Little one, you go to bed, and Aunt will bring you something nice and hot to drink as soon as the water boils." She shooed the young boy out the door, and then she turned to Lee, "Put him in bed and then come back. I will have soup for him by that time."

Lee went after his brother. In the small bedroom he found the cupboard with the sleeping mat, and the quilts. Yung Sin undressed quickly, and climbed into the warm bed made up on the floor. Leaving the light on, Lee went back to the kitchen and got a steaming bowl of thin barley broth.

"When you have fed the boy, come back and have some saki with us," his aunt said. He grinned at her wink, and hurried to finish his job.

Coming again into the little kitchen, he stopped short and

burst into a roar of laughter. His mother was standing self-consciously across the room wearing one of Aunt's dresses. The effect was very funny for the dress had been cut short and full to accommodate Aunt's squat figure. It looked ridiculous hanging on the taller, much thinner Choo.

"Now don't you laugh at your mother," Aunt said as she poured three little cups of the pungent rice wine. Steam rose from the jug in fragrant waves that filled the room with its acrid aroma. As each drank, the warm fluid spilled through their bodies driving out the damp chill. The heavy earthen walls of the kitchen muffled the sounds of guns that boomed softly in the nearby city, and in the dim, warm light, the room seemed cozy and secure. Choo drank quickly, not protesting, as she usually did, when her cup was promptly refilled by the vigilant aunt.

They sat quiet for a few minutes soaking up the warmth, then Aunt said, "We must plan." Her round face was thoughtful. "We must plan carefully if you are all to live." She sipped her wine slowly. "Now you are probably safe. It is probable that you will be able to go back to your house tomorrow and not be in danger."

"But they say the Communists . . ." Choo protested, fear crowding out her reason.

" 'They say,' Bah! Remember when the Japanese were in

our country? They used to tell us that when the Americans came they would eat us. Do you remember? We all stood in fear and trembling of the Americans, fully expecting to be eaten by them. Ah, my gullible one, just remember that the Communists are only men. And I know men if I know nothing else. I can recall one time when . . ."

"Please," Choo protested delicately, "not in front of . . . ," she motioned to Lee.

"Mmmm." Aunt nodded winking again at Lee, her black eyes sparkling in the folds of fat that enveloped them. "Yes. But I am certain that if we are careful, they will leave us alone. Eventually you will go south to your mother's farm. I am going to Taegu when it is safe. I have a house there from my second husband. In the meantime, we must watch and wait for our opportunity."

"But my husband?" Choo asked fearfully.

"It is not so with him. If they catch him, there will be no hope. They are ruthless and cruel. They stamp out anyone that might oppose them. Unfortunately they will probably know that he worked with the government here in Seoul. The informers will tell on him. He was only a little man, but they will mark him for death. He must get away. They won't be organized for a day or so, so he should have the time he needs."

"Then I can see him once more?"

"Does he know you are here?"

"He will know that we would come here if we couldn't leave the city. He will check before he leaves for the south," Lee said.

"Ah, good. I am far enough out of the city so that he will be safe here. He will need money before he goes, and extra clothes. In times like these, everything becomes very expensive. Many will want to make a profit, even though they may die tomorrow."

Lee looked at his fat little aunt as she briskly poured her fourth cup of saki. She had always been his favorite. Her humor was sharp and spicy, and she did not exclude him from her jokes. She made him feel a part of the adult world that was so separate from the growing child's world in Korea. She did not demand the polite ceremony used to address elder relatives. When he tried to use this method of speaking to her, she would often explode in impatience, telling him to get on with his story.

Lee knew only a little of her past life, of her two former husbands, but rumor had helped to fill in the gaps and while the picture was a trifle lurid, it made her seem more human than his formal relatives with their ceremony and their endless secrets from him. He could feel the warm reassurance that seemed to emanate from her, encompassing him. The earlier tensions relaxed as his head nodded forward.

"Ha," Aunt's voice brought him back, "the little man nods into sleep like an old papa-san beside the evening fire." Aunt bounced to her feet as he tried to push away the fatigue. "Come," she called from the doorway. "Tomorrow we will be very quiet. Sleep as long as you wish. Now we can only wait and see what path the storm takes before we make further decisions." She smiled gently at Lee. "Come, I will show you where to sleep." He climbed to his feet, touched his mother's cheek for a moment with his hand saying, "Do not worry." Then he followed the aunt's squat figure down the narrow central hall to a bedroom. She helped him lay out the bedding, then said in a whisper, "It is up to you now, isn't it?" She peered into his face. "Do you think that you can take care of things for a while?"

"I don't . . . yes. Yes, I can." He looked directly at his aunt.

She flapped her hand at him and said brusquely, "Of course you can. You have more good sense than many who are far older. I know you can do this job. Now sleep." She patted his shoulder and went out, sliding the door closed behind her.

The sun was high when Lee awoke. He jumped up feeling guilty because he had slept so long. After folding the bedding up, he glanced out of the partly open windows. The many panes caught the June sunlight that flooded the small room. He could still hear the distant guns just as he had heard them last night, only now they were coming from the south. The Communists must have swept through the city in the night. With the poorly equipped South Korean army in full flight, there would be very little to stop the enemy. The Communist armies might sweep their way to Pusan before any resistance could be offered. Then it would be too late. The enemy would control Korea. After such a short time of freedom to be conquered again by another people.

Lee's hands clenched into tight fists as he said, "I will never give in to them. They shall never conquer me. Never." He was startled by the sound of his voice speaking so savagely aloud. He picked up the folded bedding, and jammed it angrily into the carved wooden cupboard near the window. "If I could only do something to help." He pushed the window wide open, and the smells of moist earth and of new growth engulfed him. From somewhere outside, he could hear his brother playing. For a moment he wished that he could rush outside as he used to so long ago, and lose himself in the world of aimless imagination that children knew. It would be nice to play at the game of war, conquering non-existent cities, beating shadow enemies.

He shook his head and padded barefoot down the hallway to the kitchen. Stepping down onto the cold earth floor, he peered at the stove to see what was there for breakfast. Just then his aunt toddled in the door smelling of soap and clean clothes. "Ah, there you are. We have been washing clothes in the yard." She brushed a few unruly strands of hair back, "Such a beautiful day." She went to the stove, and, squatting before it, investigated the contents of the pots that were bubbling steamy breaths.

Quickly Aunt set dishes before Lee, and served his breakfast, her eyes darting looks at his face all the while. When he had begun to eat she said, "Such an angry face you bring to your morning meal." She clucked, filling a large brass bowl with fluffy rice. After ladling a spicy meat sauce over the rice, she placed it in front of him. He sniffed eagerly at the aromatic food, and without hesitation, plunged in hungrily. As his stomach filled, his anger faded. Drinking quick sips of tea, he leaned back and smiled at his aunt.

She beamed happily, "Ah, just like all men. Give them a good meal, and their worries disappear like mist in the morning sun. Have a little more?" She stood up.

Lee quickly shook his head. "No, I'm full." He got up, stretched, patting his full stomach, and walked over to the kitchen door. It stood open, and he could see the fields, yellow-green in the late June sunlight stretching to the low, rolling, blue foothills in the distance. The peace of the scene did not reach his heart. Still looking over the land, he asked, "Aunt, what am I going to do?" Turning to her, he repeated his question watching her face screw into tight, watchful lines. "I am too young for the army, and we are being beaten badly. There seems to be no way to stop the enemy. I want to help, but I don't know how."

"I know how you feel. Yes, I know."

"When I woke up this morning I was angry because there seemed to be nothing that I could do to help. I heard the guns in the south, and it frightened me. I know that if I went to join the army, they would take me, as they need every man. But what good would one more running man do?" Lee sat down on the doorstep, drawing his knees up under his chin.

"You can help," Aunt spoke gently. "There is much to be done beside the fighting. You are right, a few men more or less won't turn the tide of battle. Rifles are no good against tanks." Lee looked up at her wondering where she had gotten her information. "Yes, they are using tanks against us. A friend of mine came from the city this morning while you slept. He told me what he had seen. They have many fine weapons. Your brother is in the army, and your mother is worried about him. He can handle the fighting for the family. Your job is just as important. Someone who is wise and dependable must take care of the family after your father escapes. Someone who is strong must hold the family together. You can be that someone if you want to be. I know that you can take care of them. You are like me. You have good sense and a quick mind. There will be work for you to do later for your country."

"But my mother still thinks of me as a child."

"Mothers are the last people on earth to realize how fast a child grows into a young man. They want to keep their children young. To her you are still her baby. But you know what you can do. I know it. That's why I spoil you." She stood up. "One can spoil safely only very special people, you know."

"What do you mean?" Lee didn't understand her.

"It is difficult to explain, but I think that I spoil you because I know it will not change you. You will still be a good man just as you were a good child. My indulgence does not hurt you, and it gives me so much pleasure." She started out into the yard saying over her shoulder, "Now we have had our talk. I think you know what to do, so enough talk. Let's see what work there is to be done."

Lee followed the ample figure tracing her words over again in his mind. More or less, they were the echo of what his father had said. His work with the family was the most important thing that he could do now. It was his job to make sure that they were taken care of. When they were safe, then he could take the opportunity to plunge into activity. Only then could he risk himself, when he knew that they would be safe whatever befell him. Yes, he must wait before he could become part of the war. Now the important things were his family's safety, and his father's peace of mind. Firm in his new purpose he walked out into the dazzling sunlight, a smile on his face for Choo. She looked up as they came across the yard. Steam from the big tub filled with soapy water wreathed around her face, and the smoke from the fire underneath the pot filled with clothes made her cough. She stepped back to catch her breath laughing a little as she saw the warm light in her son's eyes.

Late that night Lee's father came. He slipped in the door, surprising them. Choo cried out at the sight of her husband as though she were seeing a ghost. She ran to him and they clung together for a long moment.

"Are you all right?" Mr. Lee's eyes searched Choo's face. She nodded unable to speak. "And my sons?" He looked at Lee, and seemed relieved when his son nodded that all was fine. "Why did you not leave yesterday?" Lee told his father what had happened.

"Ah, then you did the right thing. I knew you would do what was wise. You are a good man, my son."

A wonderful pride rose in Lee at this praise. His father sat down, and Choo knelt at his feet watching his face. Her eyes were wet with tears as she spoke softly, "And you, my husband, have you been safe?"

"Oh yes, I have been very careful. Before the Communists came, we managed to destroy many records. Perhaps I will be safe in the city now. There is very little left that links me to politics. I saw to that." He leaned back closing his eyes. "I am very tired. We were up all night." He looked again at his family. "I had a man watch our house, and so far the police have not been there. We will check again tomorrow. If there is still no sign of them, I think that it will be safe for us to go home. The Communists have taken many prisoners. Perhaps they are all finished, now." He drank gratefully the steaming tea that Aunt brought.

"Oh, I hope that we will be left in peace," Choo said.

"Father, are you going to stay with us at home?" Lee asked the question fearfully. He did not think that there would be safety while the Communists were in Seoul.

"Just overnight. I think that I may be more valuable in the South. The government will try to regroup there, and they will need all the men who have gotten away. I have a friend who will help me escape. We have a boat hidden that will get us across the river." The confidence in his father's voice made Lee feel much better.

"I will work my way south very slowly. I shall have to stay near the hills, and travel only at night until I am beyond the enemy. It shouldn't be too hard. Tomorrow when we go to the house, I will get money, and I will take some gold. I think that gold will be worth more than paper money in these times." He rubbed a weary hand over his eyes.

Aunt spoke up then saying, "That is all tomorrow. Right now you must sleep. I have your room prepared, as I thought you might be coming. Sleep now, and tomorrow you will feel much better." They all stood up, and Aunt led the way to where they would sleep.

The next day there was a visitor. He and Lee's father talked for a long while. When the visitor left, Lee went to his father asking, "Is everything all right?"

He was happy when his father nodded and answered, "Yes, all is well, and if there are no new reports during the day, we will return to the house early tonight."

"Father," Lee searched for the right words. "I just want you to know that I am going to take care of everything after you leave. I don't want you to worry."

"You have brought much happiness to my heart in the past, my son. Now you bring me peace." He leaned back against the wall. His gray suit was wrinkled and smudged with soot. It smelled of smoke, and burning paper. He brushed at the soot absently, saying, "I think I know what you have been feeling. It is not easy to fight the war fever that burns in the blood during times like these. You are old enough and wise enough to fight for Korea. I am happy to see that you will consider that only after our family is safe. What you have said satisfies my mind." Mr. Lee smiled at his son, saying half seriously, "You have had to grow up so fast. These are strange times. I can remember when I was your age. I followed my family's rule completely. They selected my life's work, they told me whom I should marry. How things change." Mr. Lee shook his head. "But you seem to be the first in this family to change. I can remember when we began calling you Lee. Do you recall that?"

Lee nodded his head. The incident had taken place three years ago. The family had gone to Nam San Park for a picnic. After a large lunch, Lee had wandered down the many flower-bordered walks. Turning a corner, he came on an

American lieutenant taking pictures. As this was the first time Lee had seen an American so close, he felt a little frightened. Before he could make up his mind to run off, he was noticed. The soldier turned and said in Korean, "Do not be afraid. I am taking pictures to send back to my country. I want them to see how beautiful your land is." The lieutenant rolled up the film to the last shot and asked, "May I take your picture?" He looked expectantly at Lee.

"Will my picture go all the way to America, too?"

"It sure will," the American said in English, then, remembering, he translated his answer into Korean. Lee nodded happily, and struck a pose. The shutter clicked, and for a moment, Lee felt immortal. The soldier removed the film, pasted the loose end, and put it into a leather bag that hung by a long strap over his shoulder. "What is your name?"

"Lee, Yung Chang."

"I know that in this country the last name comes first. But I like Lee as a first name. May I call you that?"

"Yes. You have been in Korea long?" Lee was certain that only a long-time resident would know these things about his country.

"No, only a few months. But I have been learning as much as I can. I want to be able to tell my people about you when I go back. Most Americans know very little about Korea."

Just then Lee saw his father coming. "My father is looking for me. Would you like to meet him?"

"Very much, if he will not consider me presumptuous," the soldier answered. Lee thought for a moment, but could not figure out what presumptuous meant. He was certain that everything would be all right. "Come," he said, "I will introduce you. What is your name?"

"Lt. Williford. You may call me Bob, since you let me call you Lee. How's that?" The last two words were in English. Lee didn't have time to puzzle about them long, for his father came up to them.

"Yung Chang, where have you been? We have been looking everywhere." He shook his head in mock irritation.

"Father may I present Lt. Williford. He took my picture and is going to send it to America." The words rushed out of Lee.

"How do you do," Lee's father spoke in heavily accented English. He looked relieved when Lt. Williford answered in Korean.

"He calls me Lee, because he likes that name better than Yung Chang." Lee spoke proudly.

Mr. Lee smiled at him saying, "Ah, I see." Turning again to the lieutenant, he asked, "Would you care to share our

lunch with us? We have eaten but it would give me pleasure
to have you join us."

But the lieutenant had to leave. "I must return to my company. Perhaps another time." They shook hands again, and
the lieutenant walked away. He turned at the corner of the
path and waved back shouting, "Good-by. Good-by, Lee."

That was how it had begun. Slowly everyone began to call
Yung Chang Lee, until it seemed that it had been this way always. Even his parents had conceded. Soon they only used his
first name when they were angry, and that was not often.

In the shadows of early night, they went back to their
house. Turning into the narrow alley, they almost ran into
one of their neighbors, Mr. Lim.

"Ah, Mr. Lee." He nodded to Choo. "I saw your house
dark, and thought that the Communists had gotten you. You
must be very careful." He hurried past them and disappeared
into the twilight.

"I do not like that man." Mr. Lee moved quickly down the
alley and opened the front door. "I wonder if he was trying to
warn me? I think that I will leave tomorrow at the earliest
possible time."

Later, as Choo prepared for the morning meal, Mr. Lee

sat smoking, sitting on the doorstep to the garden. The strong tobacco smell mingled with the scent of flowers and touched Lee's nostrils, calling up memory of many nights like this. He sat down quietly near his father. They did not speak, preferring to listen to the night sounds that drifted in on the heavy air. Beside Mr. Lee, wrapped in a silk handkerchief, was a little bundle of gold objects, rings, Choo's hair ornaments, a watch. These were the things that would buy Mr. Lee's way to the South.

Choo came out of the kitchen, her soft slippers almost noiseless on the floor. "I have finished. Everything is ready for tomorrow." She sat down beside her husband saying to Lee, "And now it is time you were in bed." They said good night, and Lee reluctantly went to his own room.

He lay sleepless listening to the sound of his parent's murmuring voices. The words were indistinct until he heard his father say, "No. Now it is too late for us to leave the city together. We would not get very far. They will have police and soldiers everywhere." Choo's voice spoke softly in answer. Again Lee could hear his father as he said, "I know. I did not want the child born to this time either. But there is nothing we can do now. How much more time do you have?"

A baby! Lee felt shock course through his veins. He strained to hear the time it would come, but the words were lost. A baby! His fingers tightened into the blanket that covered him. What would he do? He stayed for a long time staring into the dark. Many questions crowded in disorder through his mind. But there were no answers. He could only do the very best job that he was capable of. Only then would he live up to the immense trust that his father was putting in him. Holding on to the thought of how his father felt, his faith in him, Lee fell asleep.

The next morning, as they finished a hurried breakfast, there was a loud knock at the door. Mr. Lee stiffened, and then, before Choo could get up from the table, Mr. Lee thrust the silk handkerchief containing the gold into Lee's pocket. He motioned Choo to answer the door. She opened it to find two uniformed soldiers flanking Mr. Lim. He spoke almost pleasantly, "Good morning, Choo. Is your husband home?" His eyes darted beyond her, seeing the children and Mr. Lee. "Ah, there you are, Mr. Lee. You are wanted at headquarters." The man's voice became harsh, his eyes cold as he said, "You will come at once."

Choo held her husband's arm tightly, fear stark and bright in her eyes. Lee went to his father, and Mr. Lee's hand touched his son's face as he said, "Now it is for you to know, and to do."

They were gone as quickly as they had come. Lee ran out

into the alley. At the entrance, a jeep sat with running motor. The two soldiers hurried Mr. Lee to the vehicle, and they pulled away with a roar.

"It has happened. He is gone." Choo said the words quietly, but there were tears in her eyes.

"I will follow them. They will let him go. He has done nothing to them, nothing. They must let him go." Fear pounded in Lee's brain.

"No. He is gone. He will never come back. Never," Choo sank slowly down to the doorstep saying the last word over and over again. "Never, never, never . . ."

Lee turned and ran up the alley. He would go and watch. They would let his father go. Why would they want to keep him? He was only a little man. He turned the corner to the street. Faster, faster, he ran up the steep hill to the Yong San district office. Lee sat down on the curb across the street from the building.

After many minutes he looked up and down the street. How different it was. Here it was eight-thirty in the morning, and still not a person was on the street. None of the stalls or shops were open. All was silence, watchful, waiting silence. Hours began to pass. Trucks and jeeps came periodically to the station bringing new prisoners. Some of the men were grim-faced and silent, others were pleading, explaining, shouting.

Hunger told Lee when it was noon. He leaned against the linden tree that shaded him. So long ago he had played here. He closed his eyes feeling tears very close. He looked up the hill. At the top, strung across the road, he could see a red and white banner which the Communists had been quick to put up. The writing said *Peace Has Come to Seoul*. He stared at it for a long time as it waved, slowly rippling in the afternoon breeze.

Truckloads of soldiers began roaring by. The men were laughing and singing. They carried their rifles carelessly, the way men do when they have used guns so much that they are not afraid of them any more. To the south Lee could hear the incessant booming of the enemy guns. They were growing fainter and fainter.

Dark, the linden tree shadow crept longer and longer across the dusty street. Lee stood up stiffly. The familiar smells of burning charcoal, and cooking food let him know that it was supper time. He kicked a tiny gray pebble lying in the road, as he looked again at the ominous graystone building across the street. At that moment the front doors opened, and his father, between two new guards, was hurried down

the steps. Lee raced across the street standing a little way
from the jeep. They passed by him.

"Father," Lee said softly. His father's eyes touched his for
a moment, and that was all. Lee saw the trickle of blood that
ran from his father's nose, the angry, red welts on the back of
Mr. Lee's neck. The soldiers climbed in on either side. The
driver shot the jeep into gear and with a jolt it sped away in a
cloud of dust.

"Father," Lee whispered as the jeep disappeared over the
top of the hill, under the Communist slogan, *Peace Has Come
to Seoul.*

The street was quiet and darkening. Lee turned and slowly
walked back toward his house.

II The White Tiger

THE FIGHT to live began. Lee went out early one or two mornings a week to sell some family treasure at Mr. Ko's shop. Mr. Ko was the moneylender, and an old friend of the family. He often gave Lee more than he gave his usual customers. But, when Lee would go from Mr. Ko's shop to the market place, he would find that there were only a few vegetables left for sale. Rice was becoming more and more scarce as the Communists confiscated all that had been stored in Seoul. Lee went in desperation into the hills and meadows beyond Seoul to gather wild berries or dig dandelion greens. Many times whatever he brought home was all that they had to eat.

A happy day came when Lee, searching through one of the cupboards, found two pillows. He remembered that these were stuffed with some kind of grain, and that they had been used when he was a child on the hot summer nights because they were cool. He carried them to his mother.

"Oh, but you don't want me to tear these up?" Choo stroked the satin cloth. "They were used by you and your brothers when you were babies. I cannot do that," she wailed.

"They kept us cool when we were babies. Now they will do double service and keep us fed for a few days." Lee spoke practically. "Make a soup from them. That will last the longest. You can throw in the things I brought from the hills this morning."

"It will taste horrible," Choo said sullenly. "You will tell me what a terrible cook I am when you eat that . . . that . . ." Words failed her, and she made a disgusted gesture at the pillows.

"At least we will be alive to comment on the cooking," Lee answered her with a finality in his tone that allowed no arguing.

The days passed, and time became blurred. Preoccupied

with their struggle from day to day, they were not aware of Seoul except when unusual circumstances intruded on their lives. There came a night when Mr. Lim returned. They had not seen this man since he had come to take Mr. Lee away. When Choo opened the door she clutched the edge for support. Mr. Lim spoke quickly, impersonally, as though to strangers.

"There is a people's work committee forming to help with the defenses of Seoul. Your son will accompany them. I would suggest that he not offer resistance as that will be taken by headquarters as an insult to the people's government."

Lee took his jacket without a word, and followed Mr. Lim out the door.

"Be careful," were Choo's only words.

"I will," Lee whispered as he passed her. "Those hounds will not hold me." He hissed the words venomously, his eyes narrow, flat. And then, quickly shifting his expression to blankness he joined the straggling line of boys out on the street. Here and there in the group a friendly face nodded to him, but they knew better than to speak. At a command from one of the Communist guards, they walked toward the river.

The wet mud along the river's bank glistened in the truck lights that were trained on the area where they would be dig-

ging trenches. Shovels were distributed, and accompanied
by the barked orders of the many guards on duty there, they
began to work. The thick mud was heavy, and before long
Lee felt his muscles aching with fatigue from long disuse,
and from inadequate food. But he would not weaken in front
of those toads. The guards paced up and down a few feet
away, shouting abuse at the boys who were not working fast
enough.

For two hours they worked. Then the guards began to
chatter excitedly among themselves. Lee stood up, watching
them as they gestured and their voices grew louder. A few of
the Communists ran towards the truck, and the rest followed.
The trucks with grinding roars backed away from the river's
edge, turned, and sped down the road to Seoul. Lee clutched
his shovel, leaped out of the trench and ran up the steep
bank to the road. He stopped for a second, his ears straining to hear above the babble of voices behind. The other
boys began running back toward Seoul, happy to be re-
leased. Lee stood there listening. Then he heard it, as the
guards must have. A distant hum, far away, but growing
perceptibly louder, louder. The deep throated mosquito hum
coming closer . . . Lee closed his eyes, the sick fear bubbling up inside of him making him weak.

Somewhere in the night sky, a fleet of planes was moving

swiftly on a mission of death. There was no safe place to hide. In minutes, bombs would be dropping on Seoul. Where could he go? Trying to see through the velvet, warm night, he made out a dark group of trees on a knoll just a few yards off the road. He forced his shaking legs to carry him those few yards. The trees would offer some protection, but there was no way to know where the bombs would drop. If this was the night that they were going to destroy the pontoon bridges the Communists had thrown across the river, then he would die. He remembered a line from a poem he had memorized in school, ". . . for where can birds hide when there is dan ger in the sky."

The hum above him grew louder, increasing to a roar. The sound vibrated through him, making his body tingle. The planes passed overhead, flying low. Moments later came the familiar multi-whine of many bombs whistling toward earth. He dropped to the ground automatically, as explosion after explosion came from the nearby city. He felt the shock of the concussions, and the fear welled up in him drowning his brain in its black horror. He writhed helplessly, not feeling his face grind into the wet earth, not feeling the mud that squished between his clutching fingers as roar after roar battered against his screaming mind.

He didn't know how long he had been there. Time was a

lost, forgotten thing, and all that was left was the black night and space. Lee crawled forward against the tree, pulling himself to his feet. Leaning against the rough bark, his shaking hands scraped at the mud that coated his face. Even breathing was hard and came in short ragged gasps.

Why . . . why was this happening?

He rocked back and forth on his feet, trying not to fall. Tears pushed their way over the mud and coursed down his cheeks. He sank back to the ground weeping, weeping. Then he was quiet.

Slowly the night sounds came through his anguish. The scraping of cicadas, the wind rustling through leaves above his head, the murmur that was the unchanging night came seeping into his brain. Through the mud smell he became aware of the sharp pine scent around him, the heavy sweetness of wild honeysuckle and primroses. Slowly the roar in his mind stilled, the torrent of his blood slowed. He let the sounds and smells touch him and moving away from the tree, he became a part of the night, of the odors. Lee looked up through the dark to the lighter sky where the stars were strewn in muted brilliance across the limitless space plain. And seeing each gleaming speck, he felt part of them.

As he walked back toward Seoul, he drew the night into him, becoming calm.

When he arrived home, his mother embraced him, ignoring the mud, clinging to him with all her strength.

"I thought something had happened to you," she cried. He shook his head, and gently helped her to a chair. He was relieved to see that the bombs had not fallen on this part of Seoul.

"Were you all right during the raid?" he asked as he went to the window, and looked out towards the red glare that lightened the sky over downtown Seoul. Lee heard his mother's answer, and a great weariness began to flow through him. Turning he asked if there was anything that he could do for her before washing and going to bed. She shook her head, and he softly said good night.

One morning when Lee went to the moneylender's shop, he was surprised to find the man in a state of high excitement. Mr. Ko motioned Lee into the rear of the store, and whispered, "I have heard from the South." His bent frame shook with the importance of his news. "The troops have held their ground near Pusan. With the help of the United Nations, they have begun to drive the enemy back."

"Where did you hear this? Is it true?" Lee felt a new hope rising in him. Somehow he had known that this would happen. He had known it.

"A friend came through the lines from Pusan. Even now his news is old. Who can say what has happened there in the ten days that he was on the road?" The old man chortled in glee.

"They will come to Seoul. I know it. They will drive the enemy before them back to North Korea," whispered Lee in triumph.

"Ah, then your knowledge is greater than mine. Where I only hope, you know, eh?" The old man's face crinkled into a warm smile. He had come to know Lee very well in the last few weeks, and he had a kind regard for him. Often they would delay the business until they had covered all the latest news of the city, and the war. Mr. Ko was a wealth of information, as many scraps and bits filtered down to him from every corner of Seoul. His reputation for fair dealing brought him customers from even the distant farms outside of the city, and with them came a knowledge of much the enemy was hiding from the people.

Mr. Ko grew serious as he spoke again. "You must be very careful now. The enemy will take every available man to fight for their miserable cause. It will not matter how old you are, and you have added a year of age for every month you have been in this war. You must tell me, one day what has happened to make you age this way. I suspect that they are no ordinary experiences." His eyes scanned Lee's face for a moment, then he resumed. "The other day they invited all young men in the city to see an exciting motion picture. Many men went, and young boys, too. They were shown a standard propaganda film, and then a speech was made from the stage of the theater asking all present to join with the Communists to fight for the glorious cause. There were guards at each door with machine guns. The speech was quite persuasive. I understand that all present joined the army with only one exception. One man, not seeing the point, went outside with the others, but, instead of getting on the waiting trucks, he ran. Of course he was shot down. Be sure that you do not fall for any of their tricks. Be very careful. And, if I were you, I would not come here any more. Send your younger brother. Only he would be safe on the streets. You go into hiding. Have your mother tell all of her aquaintances that you have left Seoul. In that way the police and the traitors will leave your family in peace."

Lee nodded at this advice. He would follow it. "But," he said to the old man, "how can I send my young brother? Only I know how to bargain with you. You are a hard man." He laughed at Mr. Ko's expression.

"Ah! You are mad. I am the most gentle and honest of persons to deal with." He calmed a little, realizing that Lee was not serious. "Do not worry. I will take care of little brother. Send him from now on." Then his smile disappeared as Lee brought out a silver bowl to sell, and they began the highly enjoyable art of haggling.

Lee could feel the difference in the city as he left the moneylender's shop and began to pick his way homeward through the ruins. There was a new feeling in the air, an ominous air of foreboding that hung over the rubble-strewn streets. He saw it in the secret looks of the women who hurried by him, in the truckloads of soldiers that sped, horns honking imperiously through the streets. The soldiers' faces were grim, not laughing with the old arrogance. Lee darted around the ruins, keeping to the back streets as often as he could.

When he got home, he stuffed the money he had gotten into a tin box that they kept in the bomb shelter he and his brother had dug under the back bedroom floor.

"Yung Sin, where are you?" he called. The scamper of feet came across the yard, and his brother ran in the door. "Where is our mother?" Lee asked.

"She has gone to the fortuneteller's house. She wanted the future of the new child cast," Yung Sin gasped, out of breath.

"Such foolishness. It is near her time. She should not be out on the streets." Lee was worried, and it made him speak angrily. "You stay here, and I will go bring her back." He went out to the mouth of the alley. The street seemed quiet. If he ran, he would be able to get to the fortuneteller's house without being seen by too many people. She only lived a few doors away. He looked up and down the street, then ran to the alley entrance near the photographer's shop. Before he turned in, he saw a truckload of soldiers brake to a stop at the foot of the street, and they began jumping down. He stood for a second watching the men, moving quickly, rifles held ready, spread out through the little alleys that wound off the main street. They were searching house to house for something. He raced down the alley, and pounded heavily on the door of the last house. An old crone of a woman, her face crumpled into thousands of wrinkles, her thin lips shaking over toothless gums, hissed her fear when she saw who it was.

"Go away. Only women come to my house. I want no trouble with the police . . ." Her words were stopped short when Lee shoved the door open, slipped in, and started down the hallway. Entering a room heavy with smoke, he saw his mother sitting before a chart with many strange signs on it scrawled in thick black ink. She looked up at the interruption.

"But you have not removed your shoes before entering this house . . ."

"The soldiers are coming. They are searching every house probably looking for men to put in the army."

"Oh, no!" Choo raised her hand as though to ward off a sudden blow.

"They will try to take me. I don't have time to hide." Lee looked around the room quickly. There was no way out.

"You will get me into trouble." The old fortuneteller came into the room and was tugging at his sleeve. "Don't let them find you here. Let them take you in the street."

"Get me what I ask, old crone." Lee snapped at her, "Do just as I say or I will tell them that you often hide people here, and that you are working against them." The old woman looked at him with hate and fear in her eyes. Lee gave her quick orders, and she, muttering the while, hurried to fulfill them. They could hear the sound of the soldiers calling to each other coming closer and closer.

The fortuneteller hurried in with a bundle and hurled it at Lee, glaring balefully while he slipped into the clothes.

A heavy thumping knock came from the outside door. The old woman gasped in alarm. Lee hurried frantically. "Go answer it. Look just as usual, and you will be safe."

Moments later heavy feet pounded down the hall, and a red-faced soldier stood in the door, his rifle ready. He saw what appeared to be two women waiting for their fortunes to be cast. Lee smoothed the long woman's dress down to make sure that his booted feet did not show, and he drew the heavy shawl closer around his face, not looking at the soldiers. Choo, controlling her shaking voice, called out impatiently, "Old grandmother, come finish our fortunes. My daughter and I have to get back to our house." The soldier came a little closer, and Choo leaned over studying the signs on the chart, her body throwing Lee into deeper shadow. The fortuneteller came in behind the soldier, and her familiar whine seeped into the room, "I am a good woman. I have done nothing wrong." The soldier turned, "All right old woman. I am going." He clomped out. The fortuneteller followed him to the door, and Lee heard it close noisily.

He saw Choo's shoulders shaking, and he leaned toward her saying, "It is all right. They have gone, now. Don't cry." Then he saw that Choo was not crying, she was laughing.

"You look so silly," she howled loudly. The old fortuneteller came in and said crossly, "Keep up that unseemly howling and you will have all of us killed." Lee chuckled as he slipped out of the disguise, "I see now what my father meant when he said that there was more than one way to fight a war."

Going home they could see that the soldiers had worked their way up the street, and that the danger was past for the present. As they hurried down the familiar alley, Lee told Choo all that the moneylender had said earlier. She listened eagerly, and asked when the soldiers would be coming back to Seoul. Lee did not know, as the information was only slight. Choo's face grew troubled, "That means that war is going to come back to our city. Only this time the might of the world will be passing through." She stopped. "I wonder if any of us will be alive by the time it is over?" Her eyes looked at their house, so frail when bombs started falling. It would seem that a small bomb could blow the stone and wood structure to bits with no trouble. She looked over to the neighbors' houses clustered at this end of the alley. They stood gray and blank, showing no signs of life.

"I wonder what our home will look like when it is all over." Choo spoke almost to herself. "When we are able, I think that we should go to my mother's farm down south. There we will at least have enough to eat. The enemy probably will not bother farmhouses as much as they will city places." She started up the two muddy steps to the front door.

"Yes. You need enough to eat, especially now. Tell me, Mother, when is the child due?"

"If you promise me not to worry, I will tell you when the baby will come." Choo waited for his nodded assent. "I will have the child at the end of September. I tell you this because your quick thinking today shows me that you are more a man than a child. It will be a hard time." She held up her hand, not letting him interrupt. "If we make careful plans, it will be well. I will tell you what you may do before the time comes. You will have only a small part in the delivery, as all of my friends here will be able to take care of me very well." She saw the worried frown on Lee's face and said, "Do not fear for me. I am strong, and I have become used to having children."

"But you aren't strong. You . . ."

"Shhhh. I am fine." She turned and went into the house. Lee, stifling the fear that was always with him, followed her, calling loudly for his younger brother. Now would be the time to tell Yung Sin that he would be going to the money-lender's shop from now on.

He instructed the boy on the fine art of bargaining with the moneylender, but insisted that Yung Sin always be polite. "You must remember that you are much younger than Mr. Ko. It would be unseemly for you to become angry with him. I think that if you maintain proper respect, you will find him quite easy to work with."

The first time that the younger brother went to the money-lender's shop, he came back with his eyes sparkling with excitement. "I saw the soldiers, and they were all together in the square. A big general was standing in the back of a truck making a speech to them. I couldn't understand much that he said, but I think that he was telling them to fight hard, and to be brave." Yung Sin reached into his pocket and pulled out a thick roll of money. "Look, I got all this for the watch." Lee took the money and counted it quickly. It was a lot, and he understood what Mr. Ko had meant when he said that he would take care of them.

"But why do we have to buy so much food?" Yung Sin asked loudly. "There are many gardens beyond the main city that I passed that were full of vegetables. They just lie there for the taking. Why not go out at night and pick up some? No one would miss a few." His face reddened as he spoke, because he knew that what he was asking was wrong. Lee did not know what to say. He had often thought of that himself. It would be a simple matter to add to their short food supply at the expense of someone else's garden.

Choo was sitting by the window sewing, and she paused to listen to the youngster speak. When he had finished she looked for a long moment at her sons, and then she said, "Why not? You are right, Yung Sin. It would be easy to do this thing, but even as you speak, you know that it would be wrong. You know this, both of you. If you did this it would not be honest. You would not be true to yourselves. One time, you think, does not matter. But do this once, and you

become weak so that the second time is certain to happen."
She smiled at them, breaking the stern look that had captured
her features.

"Come sit by me, my sons." She moved over to give them
room on the low wooden bench under the window. "I had
such thoughts once. There was something that I wanted very
much, and thoughts just like yours came to me. Your grandmother knew them even before I spoke. I will tell you the
story that she told me then." Choo put her sewing into the
basket at her feet. "This is a story of the old days, of the legendary kingdom in the North. It is the story of the White
Tiger, and of the man who dared to ride him.

"Many years ago, long before history was written, there
lived in the North a white tiger. Now, you know that the
tiger is the most savage animal in all Korea. But the people
said that this one was more savage than twenty ordinary
tigers. They said that he was as big as a mountain, and could
swallow a man in one gulp. Of course, no one had ever seen
the tiger, as they were all too afraid to go anywhere near him.
All men were afraid of the tiger except the king. He felt that
the white tiger was like him in many ways, for he had become
a powerful king and many people feared him. His bravery
had become legendary. As he grew older, he thought so
much of the white tiger that he had one embroidered on all

of his robes as a symbol of his greatness. He made a stamp for all of his official papers that only he might use, and that stamp was a white tiger.

"As the years passed, the stories of the king and the tiger become woven together in the people's minds, and it was hard to tell which was being described, the man or the tiger.

"When the king grew very old, he fell sick. All the statesmen gathered around his bed, and asked who would succeed him to the throne. For a long time the king would not answer, for the question made him very sad. You see, he had all that a king could desire, except for one thing. He did not have a son.

"When it was obvious that the king could not live much longer, the statesmen demanded that he make a choice. They knew that if he did not, and died, then many men would fight to claim the rich kingdom, and war would destroy it.

"The king thought and thought. He wanted an heir as strong, as good a ruler as he. He knew that this man might come from anywhere. He might be a neighboring prince, or he could be a poor man in the kingdom. How could he be found. Then an idea came to him. He called all of his advisers and ministers around him to hear. They strained forward to hear his decision. The old king spoke slowly with great effort.

" 'I want two things. I want an heir to the throne, and I want to get well. For a long time I have believed that if I could touch the white tiger, that one which is so like me, I would be well again. Then I would have time to train the man who would one day be king.'

" 'Here, then, is how you will find the man. Send a proclamation to every corner of the land and say that my kingdom will go to the one who can bring the white tiger to me.'

"All of the statesmen looked at each other. Find the symbol of the king's power and bring it to the palace? No man would dare to do that. They voiced their fears at this task. The king rested for a moment, then said, 'The man will be found. Let it be known that I am dying. Let it be known further, that the touch of the white tiger can cure me. The one who brings it to the palace will be a man who cares more for me than for his own life. He will be the one who wants me to live, not die. When I am well, I will walk among the people, and beside me the king of the future will be riding . . . riding on the white tiger.' The king slumped back, his strength spent.

"Many days passed after the proclamation had been sounded throughout the kingdom. Many men tried to become king, but they failed. Even those who seemed worthy could not find the tiger. Some were overconfident, some were frightened of the unknown. Many resorted to trickery, and they came back to the palace telling of their adventures searching for the tiger, and they told of how they had been forced to kill the animal in terrible combat. Some even had white tiger skins with them to prove their story. But always the skin proved to be a regular tiger skin painted white. One man even had a skin made of white hair sewn by master craftsmen to a tiger skin. The king ordered these men executed for their lies. As the time crept by, the king despaired of finding his successor.

"Then, one day when the king knew that he could not live any longer, he heard a great shouting. Pulling himself out of bed, he was helped over to the window. Looking down into the palace courtyard, he saw crowds of people pouring through the great iron gates. In their midst, a young man walked. Beside him strode the white tiger. The king hurried down, and when he appeared at the top of the long flight of marble stairs a silence fell over the crowd. The young man and the tiger moved up the stairs to the king. A breathless silence hung in the air, as the king moved forward slowly to meet them. The king sought the great green eyes of the beast. He felt the fire of the animal's gaze pierce him. He moved more quickly, his hands outstretched to touch.

"Then a strange thing happened. At the exact moment that the king's groping hands touched the tiger, he seemed to stand straighter, to grow younger before their eyes. In a moment, he raised his hand to the people saying, 'I am strong again. I am well.'

"Then he turned to the young man who had brought the tiger, and asked how this had come about.

" 'When the news came to my village that you were sick, my king, I knew that I must try to help you. It seemed an impossible and a frightening task when I first set out. In fact, I was afraid so that I shivered to my toes. I had no weapons other than this knife. I was not a great hunter. But when I grew most afraid, I would think of you. Saving you was the most important thing, and all else was second. When I found the tiger, I told him why he must come. All the other hunters had wanted him for their own glory. I wanted him to save you. He came with me.'

" 'Mount the white tiger. You shall ride beside me and I shall proclaim to the people that you are my heir, and that you will rule when I have done. You have shown greater courage, and greater virtue than any before.' He turned to the court scribes, 'So let this tale be written that all may learn the just reward for virtue.'

"And together they went among the people, the king, the white tiger, and the young man of virtue who dared to ride him . . ."

They were quiet for a moment at the end of the story. Choo picked up the sewing that had slid from her lap. "You see," she said, "there will one day be a chance for you to do some great and fine thing. Do not let your past mistakes or weaknesses rise like ghosts to drive opportunity from you. In your mind, in your heart prepare yourself should you one day have the chance to ride the white tiger."

III City under Siege

As AUGUST moved into September, the war took a new turn. Rumor brought news of the Inchon landing led by General MacArthur, and stories were told of how the enemy had suffered a crushing defeat in the South. Mr. Ko kept the Lees informed of the troop movements as they rapidly neared Seoul. This was the news that all the city had been waiting for. The neighbor women gathered at Lee's house to discuss it. Excitement was shining in their faces, and it was in the steady twittering of their voices. Mrs. Kim, the woman who had taken charge of Lee's mother, stopped to talk to him before joining the other women.

"They are coming soon. I can feel it. I went to the fortune-teller today, and she told me that the signs said we would be soon free."

"But it will get much worse before it gets better," Lee said quietly.

"She said that, too." Mrs. Kim peered at him through her silver-rimmed spectacles. "She said that much blood would be shed before this is all over."

"Mrs. Kim, how is my mother? Every time I ask her, she just says that she is fine, that she doesn't need anything."

"She is doing well. I don't really understand why. A woman with child needs a lot of rest and quiet. She needs good food. Choo gets none of these things. Oh, I know that you do your best, but what can you do in times like these?" Seeing that Lee was becoming more worried at her words, she hastened to add, "Of course, if your mother wasn't really strong, then I would worry. But she is made of iron. Iron. I have never seen one so strong. She will have the baby. It will be a good one, too. I know. I can tell."

Lee knew that Mrs. Kim was the best midwife in the whole district. She had helped to bring many new lives into the world, and he knew that he could trust her.

"I brought you into the world, young man." She chuckled, remembering. "Oh, I can see it so plainly." She shook her head as she glimpsed the past for a moment. "Such a fat little one you were . . . ," she laughed aloud. Then, becoming serious again she said kindly, "Do not worry. All of us here in this alley are going to help. We are here now to bring the things the baby will need, and we will take care of her through it all. You help all you can, and just watch us work." She shook her finger at him, "You will see."

The rest of the day went slowly. Lee was restless, but he dared not leave the house while the enemy still had control of the city. He wandered through the rooms of the house trying not to get in the way of the bustling women. Their endless, cheerful chatter made him nervous as they moved from the kitchen to the bedroom where his mother lay. Mrs. Lee had told him that the baby would not arrive for at least another week. He couldn't understand why all this fuss was going on so long before. Lee didn't realize that the baby was a good excuse for these women to forget the terror of their lives, to get together as they did in the old days.

Lee went into the back bedroom to check the bomb shelter again. He pulled back the mat, lifted the trap door, and jumped in. It had taken many days to dig, but it was needed for security. Lee lit a candle near the entrance, and looked around. The shelter was almost as big as the room above it, and he felt satisfaction at the way he had braced it with heavy planks from the back yard. He moved carefully so as not to hit his head on the chimney pipes that ran under the floor from the kitchen to the back outside wall. Checking the supplies, he thought that he would need more mats for the dirt floor to help keep the dampness out. The chimney pipes would supply warmth, and there were blankets to keep the chill out. He checked the water supply, tasting it for freshness.

When he had satisfied himself that all was in order, he swung up through the trap door, blowing out the candle. He slipped the trap back into place, and pulled the mat over it. A wave of pride swept him as he looked at his handiwork. It was impossible to detect the presence of a hidden room when the mat was in place.

Night came slowly. Only one or two of the women stayed with his mother. They hurried about with candles. One went into the kitchen to cook the boys' supper, and the other stayed with Mrs. Lee.

As the hour grew later, Lee stopped reading the book he had picked up after supper. He looked toward the window, listening. The sound of guns had been growing all day, but now there was an odd quiet. He blew out his candle, and went into the garden. Even the usual night sounds seemed to be still. He could hear only the sound of one woman humming as she worked in the kitchen.

From far over the horizon came a soft thump. A moment passed, and then there was the sound of rushing air. It was a weird hoarse shriek of a sound, followed by a tremendous explosion. The force of the concussion slammed Lee back against the house. Windows near him rattled almost to the breaking point. He leaped inside banging the door behind him, and raced down the corridor to his mother's room. He found Mrs. Kim and two other women wrapping Choo in blankets.

"Into the shelter! We are going to put her into the shelter," one cried. Another crash rocked the house, and some of the windows blew out, spraying glass through the room. Lee ran into the back bedroom and pulled away the mat. Lighting a candle, he tugged at the trap door, pulling it loose.

"Everything is ready," he called, jumping into the dark hole. The women hurried forward, and Choo was lifted down. When she was comfortable, Lee climbed up, and went to the kitchen. He pulled the stove door open. The fire was burning low. There was no firewood in the kitchen, only thick grass in tight bundles. He ran into the family room. There was a heavy antique chest against one wall. He tore the thick doors from it without hesitation, and ran back to the stove. The fire licked up around the splintered doors. "They will burn long and slow," he thought with satisfaction. He went back to the shelter.

The bombardment grew in intensity. Hour after hour passed, and still it did not let up. Waiting in the dark, they put out the candles to conserve them.

The earth shook with the fury of death that rained in the night. The force of the blasts shook little streams of dirt down on them as they crouched in the blackness. Yung Sin had fallen asleep near Choo. Lee was relieved that his crying had stopped. The only sound was the explosions, and the gasps of the women when one shell landed close.

After many hours, there was silence. They waited to make sure that it would last. Then Lee pulled himself up, and pushed away the trap door. Climbing over the edge of the floor, he could see that the house was still standing. Checking further, he found that all the windows had been blown out, and the plaster was severely cracked in many places. But that was all. With relief he reached down and helped Choo and Mrs. Kim up. After making certain that Choo was all right, he went to the kitchen to stoke the fire, using more of the chest to bring the fire to a bright blaze.

The women who had come to help moved dazedly about, trying to shake the ache from their bones. One began to get the morning meal, while the other prepared a tray to take to the bedroom. When it was ready, Lee took it with a smile. "I will serve her." The woman nodded silently.

Choo was sitting up, and she smiled at him, trying to hide the fearful currents that raced below the surface of her eyes.

"Here is your tray, Mother." Lee set the tray across her knees. "Is there anything else that I can do?"

"Everything is ready now. We can only wait, but I think that the time is near." She reached out and touched Lee's cheek. "Tonight, take your brother over to Mrs. Kim's house. I think that all of this noise has quickened my little one. I don't understand why, but he is becoming eager to begin his life." She smiled softly, stroking her full body saying, "Little fool, you will never be so comfortable again."

Choo looked towards the glassless windows. "We have no flowers," she said, as though realizing it for the first time. "I miss them very much. The sight of our chrysanthemums nodding out there used to give a special meaning to the autumn." Lee watched her as she leaned back wistfully turning her eyes from the ragged back yard that was overgrown with weeds which fought each other for space to live on the tiny plot. He understood what she felt. He had missed the garden, too. How good it would be to work there again with Father. How good to learn the names of the many plants, their likes, their dislikes, the treatment that each one needed to grow to its fullest beauty. Father had said that plants were like people. Each needed special understanding if it was to grow well. Lee and Choo sat there looking out into the green world beyond the window. Each was lost in thoughts of a time that was not now.

The door slid open. "And when you go over to the house, bring me some candles. You will find them in the kitchen." Mrs. Kim came into the room talking over her shoulder to Yung Sin. She turned and beamed at Choo. "Now, how are you feeling?" She went right on without waiting for an answer. "But, look. You have eaten almost nothing." She looked distressed and sat down beside Choo to feed her.

"Lee, go with your brother and see if there is any way to make that old house of mine safe for you to stay in tonight."

Lee went to the door as she continued, "I think that if you go into the root cellar under the kitchen you will be fine. But don't eat all the vegetables that are drying there, you hear?" He nodded, smiling.

Lee didn't mind Mrs. Kim's brusque tone. It made him feel better to see her energy, the quickness of her step after such a night. He went across the alley, stopping for a minute to look back at his house. In the back of his mind, he could still hear the scream of shells overhead, and the blasts that had shaken the house to its foundation. He turned away. None of them had hit. And none of them would hit tonight. He thought that again and again, as he pushed the wisps of fear away from his mind.

The night came quickly, rushed by his fearful anticipation. A warm red glow lit the horizon. A few clouds washed with gold moved slowly across the sky. Lee did not see them as he hurried across the alley to Mrs. Kim's house. The women's chatter had stilled to worried whispers. The baby still had not come. That meant it would come in the night. Even Mrs. Kim was beginning to show sharp concern. He entered her house. This waiting was the hardest part. The not knowing, the uncertainty was enough to sicken the strongest man with fear. He sat in the kitchen with Yung Sin. Looking at his small brother hunched in the corner by the stove, Lee felt a sadness well up in him. "It will be all right soon, my brother." He touched Yung Sin's shoulder. "You had better go down into the cellar and see that I did not forget anything for tonight." The young boy nodded mutely up at him, and rose to leave.

Lee watched the blue gloom spill out of the corners of the small room. Still he sat there waiting, listening. As the darkness became final, the first distant boom came, followed by the shrill whistling tear as a shell passed somewhere near.

The explosion shook the house a little, but it was quite far away. Perhaps they were going to bomb another part of the city tonight. The thought that raced through Lee's mind was soon shattered as the next explosions followed the first. The concussion made him reel against the wall. He groped his way to the opening, and slid into the cellar.

"Yung Sin, it has begun again," he whispered in the darkness. He heard the answering whimper, and he lit a candle to help the boy's fear. They looked at each other in the light of the flickering candle. The two faces were very different. Yung Sin's was fearful, tear-streaked. Lee's was almost expressionless, withdrawn. With the next near crashes, Yung Sin's eyes grew wide with animal-like terror, and he crept near Lee, and huddled there.

"Try to sleep," Lee said gently. "It will not be so bad tonight. It will be easier to sleep." Lee continued to talk, pausing when the bombs drowned out his voice. He let his mind wander, picking out bits from the pleasant past to tell Yung Sin. He remembered their trip to the Diamond Mountains when they were very young. "Remember how shining the peaks were in the morning sunlight? And how they were pointed like needles and you wanted to climb one . . . You were so disappointed when Father wouldn't let you . . ." His voice went on and on. The word pictures of pleasure and adventure seeped into his brother's mind, causing him to finally relax enough to fall asleep.

It had not been too bad while talking to Yung Sin. But now the bombardment crashed with impact after impact against Lee's mind. He sat there, numbed, rigid, as the night dragged toward the distant dawn.

It seemed as though years had passed since he had entered the cellar. He could not tell quite when the shelling stopped, but suddenly he was aware of the stillness as the silence struck through his frozen control. He moved carefully so that he would not wake his brother. Standing up, he climbed stiffly up through the narrow opening into the kitchen. His muscles and bones throbbed painfully from the night dampness that came from the earth cellar, and his legs were shaking from fatigue. The house across the alley was still. There seemed to be no life there. He stepped into the fresh morning air, and looked up at his chimney. A thin blue curl rose into the morning gray. Lee ran quickly to his kitchen door.

"Oh!" Mrs. Kim jumped up from the fire she was building. "You startled me. I thought you must be the police. You made as much noise as those bombs last night." She returned to the fire, stuffing the grass bundles through the little iron door.

"Is everything . . . has the new one come?" Lee watched the woman working slowly at the fire. As he watched, in a brief instant of wordless communication, he knew that everything was well. Not trusting his instincts, he waited for her words.

"Ah, yes. You have a fine new brother. Your mother is asleep now with the baby." Mrs. Kim stood up. "As you can imagine, it was a very difficult night. After I make everything ready, I am going to sleep." She looked closely at Lee. "I think that you had better do the same. You look as though you have been dead for several days." She pointed wearily to a place for him to sit down. "There. You sit, and we will have breakfast together. Mrs. Pahk will be here in a few minutes. She will stay all day. She can feed your brother when he wakes up."

The food was ready in a short time. Lee ate quickly, feeling no real hunger. Only a dragging weariness pulled at him, and made his eyes burn, his head light. After finishing, he thanked Mrs. Kim, and went down the hall to his mother's room. Sliding the door open, he looked in. His mother and the baby were asleep. Lee saw a tiny smile play over Choo's lips. He felt his eyes grow wet as he watched, seeing her drawn features, and the contentment that was there. He went out silently, going to his room. Without undressing, he slumped down on a mat, and fell asleep instantly.

Three days later, the guns stopped. Throughout the city, people raised their heads to listen. Only a death-like silence greeted their ears. In Lee's house, no one spoke. They sat there trying to absorb the silence . . . to find a reason. Looking at each other, they dared not speak, afraid to shatter it. Lee stood up, listening. A vague rustling came from beyond the walls. Someone was coming. He raised the trap door a few inches.

"Choo, Choo! Are you there?" It was Mrs. Kim. She yanked the trap door out of Lee's cautious fingers and shouted, "They are coming. The tanks, the army . . . They are coming." The words tumbled one over the other as she tried to tell them. Lee understood. "The Americans?" He laughed wildly at her wordless nod. The baby, wakened by the noise, began to cry lustily.

"Mother, Mother, they are here," Lee shouted, scrambling up through the trap door. "Yung Sin, do you hear? At last they have come. The monsters are driven out." He ran to the front door. Yes, he could hear it. Far away there was a deep rumble that grew louder, shaking the houses as it approached. He could hear the metal clanking of the machines, and the sound was music. He dashed back to the women. After helping Choo out of the shelter, he said, "I cannot see them from here. The turn of the alley hides them from me. I must go out."

"It is very dangerous out there now," Mrs. Kim said quickly. "The streets are not safe. I looked before coming here, and there are many dead men there. It is hard to push all the evil ones out with one blow. There are many left. They are lying out there, somewhere, waiting to kill. If you are wise, you will stay here and be safe." Mrs. Kim hurried to the kitchen calling to Yung Sin to help her fix breakfast.

Lee did not wait to hear more. He went quickly out the front door. Standing there in the early morning grayness, he could tell that the jangling roar came from the corner. It rose and fell as a tank approached and passed. They seemed to be quite far apart. He looked over his shoulder at the house, to see if anyone was watching, then he darted up the alley to the street. He stopped in the shadow of the building, and slowly peered up and down the street. There were some bodies lying at various spots, probably from earlier street fighting. The noise of the tanks was very loud, even though they were passing at the foot of the hill. All he could see was the dust that was thrown up by their great, crunching treads.

"Lee," someone called from the house. He looked back, and then turned quickly into the street. He had to see. Moving through the deep shadow of early dawn, he went quickly toward the corner. Through the tanks' noise, he became aware of the scattered sound of rifle fire, and the excited chatter of an occasional machine gun burst. As the street grew lighter, he saw more of the crumpled figures in the road. Breaking into a half run, he moved quickly nearer his destination. Across the street he heard a near rifle explode. Without thinking, he dropped to the ground just as a slug smashed into the wall above him. He rolled to the mouth of a nearby alley, and dived in, crouching in its sheltering darkness.

Whoever had fired at him would have a hard time finding the target now, he thought as he caught his breath. Moving cautiously towards the back of the building, his foot stepped on something soft, yielding. He jumped back, frightened, straining his eyes in the darkness. Through the gloom, he could make out the shape of a sprawling body. Near the dead man's hand he saw something else. Stooping quickly, he scooped up the object. It was a gun. The cold metal, heavy in his hand, made him shiver. Stuffing it into his belt, he moved slowly to the rear of the alley.

Still determined to see what was happening, he decided that a roof would be the best vantage point for observation.

The Pahk's house was near the corner, and it had a high roof. It would serve to hide him as he watched. Lee ducked through the back yards until he was behind the three-story building. The stucco ornaments and balconies offered convenient footholds as he climbed up to the top. He pulled himself over the edge, being careful to stay concealed behind the low wall that ran across the front of the building.

Slowly he raised his head to look down into the street. An awed gasp broke from him as he saw the stream of heavy tanks rolling by. The strength and power of the vehicles excited him. They were here to free his country. This might of the Western world had been sent to drive the invader out of Korea. Lee tried to see the faces of the men in the tanks. All that showed in each was one man's head cautiously poked out of the central hatch. The steel helmets that each wore low over their eyes shadowed the features so that they were obscured. Lee imagined that they all looked like the GI he had met in Nam San Park that bright day so long ago. To him it was perfectly possible that the lieutenant might be in one of the mud-encrusted machines that moved below. The thought made him smile. He looked up to the top of Nam San mountain rising out of the blue dawn mist.

Out of the corner of his eye he caught a motion on a roof across the street. At once his mind was alert, back in the present. Watching closely, he saw a figure moving towards the edge of the opposite roof, looking down at the tanks.

"Someone else wants to watch," he thought, and returned to the stream of dark machines that continued to pour by. They made such a great noise that his thoughts were blasted away. He looked again across the street to see if the man there had seen him. A gasp of horror broke from his lips.

"No!" he cried, his voice lost in the jangling roar below.

The man had crouched near the edge of the flat roof. He carried a rifle. As Lee watched, he took careful aim and fired at the tank now passing. The soldier in the hatch stiffened, slumped forward, and slowly slid out of sight into the tank. Instinctively, Lee tore the pistol from his belt. His hand was shaking so badly that he had to steady it on the roof ledge. The man across the street was taking aim again.

Slowly Lee squeezed the trigger. The gun jumped a little in his hand, but the sound of the shot was barely audible above the noise in the street. The man leaped up, his white-clothed figure sharp against the sky.

"I've missed," thought Lee wildly.

Then he saw the man tip slowly forward, hands clawing at the air, and plunge into the street below. Lee stared down at the white bundle that lay motionless in the gutter.

He crept to the back of the roof, and heavily climbed

down to the alley. He felt weak and old as he stood there in the darkness. His legs would hardly carry him toward his house.

He had done something, as he had longed to do. This should be a moment of triumph. But only the horror of his act filled him. He wanted to go home, to hide in his room. He wanted to hide from his people. Lee moved faster and faster through the back yards.

Less than two days later the GIs marched triumphant into Seoul. Cheering crowds lined the streets of the ruined city. They waved little American and Korean flags that had appeared from everywhere, and they cried out their affection to these bronzed giants riding by in trucks and jeeps.

Lee watched the parade. His hands were thrust deep into his pockets, his face was tired and grim. Yes, it was good that the enemy had been driven out, that Seoul was free again. But he could not still the ache that rose in his heart at the cost of these last months . . . his lost father, the empty house, the city destroyed. And the thought of that early morning only two days ago when he had killed a man. Like a little boy, he had run home to his mother. But the house had been throbbing with the news of the enemy's collapse. The baby commanded the center of attention for the women. He had not been noticed. That was just as well, he thought now. This was something that she should never have to know.

At that time he had needed to tell her, to hear her words of comfort and understanding. When she had moved away from him, he had gone to his room. There he wept silently, until his control returned. When he had come out of the room, his face was closed, older. The boy had died; the man was developing.

He turned from the parade, pushed his way to the edge of the shouting crowd, and walked away.

It had been many days since Lee had been in the downtown area. It was only now that he realized how extensive the damage to the city was. The change was so great, that he almost lost his way. Looking about, he could see many people scrambling over the rubble, searching. He stopped to watch a small group being spurred on by a very elderly woman. She ignored the dirt that smeared her billowing white dress, and clawed into the wreckage of what had once been a building. In a hoarse voice she ordered those with her to lift the heavy timbers while she dug with her hands at the brick and glass.

The two men must have been her sons, as they obeyed quickly. The third person was a quiet girl of about twenty. She stood to one side, resting. Her hands were badly scratched from moving the jagged stones, but her tired, dusty face showed no sign of pain. Lee turned to move on when he heard a wail come from the older woman. He turned and ran over to the group. They were huddled around a single spot. The old woman was crying aloud, and wringing her hands. Lee scrambled over the rubble, and as he drew near, he could see what had happened. They had found what they were looking for. Part of a body was now visible from underneath the clump of wreckage.

Lee helped them move away the rest of the debris that was on the body. Gently, gently they pulled the body free. It was that of a young man. His face had not been hurt, but dried blood stained the front of his shirt. Together they laid him on a level stretch of ground. The old woman fell on her knees beside him murmuring incoherent words through her tears. The young girl stood a little apart, her face blank, no expression even in her eyes. As she watched, she slowly turned the heavy gold wedding ring on her left hand.

Lee left the group and continued on toward his house. He passed the Nam Dae Moon market place as he made his way up the steep hill that rose behind Seoul.

"Lee," a voice called. He turned and saw the old moneylender scrambling over the piles of stone that had been his shop. Mr. Ko limped up to Lee and peered into his face.

"You are all right? Your family?" Mr. Ko fired the questions one after another. Lee nodded quickly, happy to see the old man safe.

"Yes, all my family is safe," Lee waved his arm at the destroyed buildings. "You, how about you? Your shop is only a pile of stone. How did you escape?"

"*Ai*. Hah, I am a tough old bird. It will take more than this to kill me." Mr. Ko chuckled without any humor. "My shop is gone, my house is gone, but I am still here. I must find a place to live." His sharp old eyes scanned the wreckage. "I must find a place, that is, if there is anything left standing in this city." He shrugged and said, "I am only grateful for one thing. I managed to bury most of my stock before the city was torn apart. At least I will be able to begin business again as soon as I am set up." He shrugged.

"We have much room at my house with my father gone and my brother off to war. Why don't you come and visit with us for a while?" Lee phrased his words very carefully. When offering help to an older person, one had to make it seem that he was doing you a favor. "You would do us a great honor. We need the advice that can only come from one whose wisdom is great."

"It is your kind heart that makes you say these things. I could not do that."

"It would be our pleasure to make you welcome." Seeing the old man hesitate, Lee said directly, "These are strange times. One must help friends when they are in trouble. Let my family do this. We will only be practicing a lesson that you taught us when the enemy was here."

The direct words were effective. Mr. Ko nodded, saying, "You are good." Then he motioned to the rubble saying, "I would pack a few things, but to get to them, I would need a steam shovel." They both laughed, and walked up over the hill to Lee's house.

Choo was in the kitchen when they reached home. Lee had the old man sit down in the family room, and then went directly to her.

"Mother, I have brought Mr. Ko to stay with us for a while." Lee told her what had happened as she worked at the stove stirring an iron pot of thin soup that would be their lunch. She nodded as she listened, reaching for another bowl and spoon.

"He is welcome to share with us. There is not much here, but he may stay as long as he likes." She pushed a loose wisp of hair back from her forehead, as she peered into the steaming pot. Her face was drawn and pale, but her movements were quick and certain.

"Mother, should you be up so soon after the baby?" Lee's worried voice made her smile.

"You sound like your father. No, it is not too soon for me to be up. There is much to do. First, I must take care of you. Mrs. Kim will help me if I get tired. Next, we must prepare."

"Prepare for what?"

"We do not have much money. There are almost no things of value left to sell. We have very little choice if we are to survive. I have planned to go to my mother's house in the South until things are more settled." She looked at him. "You know, I don't think that things are finished here. I am positive that the war will come back to Seoul. When that happens, I want to be far away."

"Yes, that could happen again. They will build up in the North. They won't give up easily." Lee thought for a moment. "We will have to arrange transportation. That will be very difficult. Many people will have the same thought."

"A farm is a good place to be in times like these. I am sure that my mother will be able to take us in. Then we will have enough to eat, and you two boys can work on the farm. In that way, all of us will benefit. I know that since your grandfather died it has been hard to get the rice crop to market. Taegu is only a few miles away, but for a woman it is too far to travel. You will be able to sell the food in town, and at the same time you can go to Aunt's house there. She will be able to help you find buyers who will pay a good price. Tomorrow you go to the train station. See what can be done."

"We may not be able to go for a long time. There will be many supplies coming in on the trains. The army will be using them most of the time. There will be very little room for passengers."

Choo gave the pot a final stir, saying, "I must go and greet our new guest. Would you prepare the table?" Lee nodded as she went into the other room to Mr. Ko. He put the brass spoons beside the bowls and moved the table into the room where they ate. As he passed the family room, he heard Mr. Ko and Choo talking warmly. It was good to hear a man's voice in the house again.

In a moment, Choo appeared in the doorway. "There, we will serve if everything is ready." She put the thin soup into a serving dish.

"Mother, what if Father comes back while we are gone?"

"I will leave a message with the neighbors. They will tell him, and he won't worry." She poured the hot liquid carefully, not looking at him. Then, putting the iron pot on the stove with a clank she said, "But he will not come back. I feel him dead. Inside me, in my heart, I know that they have killed him. A woman knows these things." She looked at him then. Her face was not sad, not anything. She was telling him the things she believed. To her these things were so. They were done. There was nothing that could now be done to change them.

"He has died," she went on, "but there is a new life in our house. Perhaps his spirit is in my new baby. They say that when a man dies, somewhere in the world a new child is born. The man's spirit enters that new child, and so he continues living. I want to believe that this is so." Choo smiled at him. "Here, enough of such talk. Take this and put it on the table. I will bring our guest." She went out to Mr. Ko again.

Lee shook his head thoughtfully. These were, indeed, strange times. He didn't understand all that his mother had said, and he didn't understand why he should be doing woman's work setting the table. He shrugged and carried the soup to the next room.

They ate quietly together for a time, then Lee asked Mr. Ko whether or not travel was possible at this time.

"I have heard that the railroads are still running. They have been jammed with refugees fleeing to the South." He paused waiting to see what they were seeking.

"We have decided to go to my mother's farm near Taegu.

I feel that would be best for all of us now," Choo said.

"I am distressed to hear of your leaving, of course, but I think that it is a wise thing for you to do."

"We shall not be able to go for a while. It will take time to get travel passes." Lee spoke thoughtfully. "I imagine that they are very hard to get, now."

"Perhaps I can help you. A friend of mine may be able to take care of your passes after a while. Not for a few weeks, though."

Choo spoke wistfully, "I would be happy if I knew that the house was in good hands while we were gone. In times like these, there are many lawless people about, and nothing is safe."

"Do you have no one you could leave to take care of the place for you?"

"I can think of no one who would want so much trouble. They would have to live here. It is a lot to ask some friend to leave their home and move here just as a favor to me."

"If I could be of help, it would be my pleasure." Mr. Ko touched his mouth with his napkin.

"I would deeply appreciate it if you would take care of things for us."

"Consider it done, please," said Mr. Ko.

Lee listened to the words that almost hid his mother's offer

to let the moneylender live in their house while they were in
the South. This was the old way of doing things in Korea. He
was pleased that his mother could help out their friend who
had no place to go. She made it seem that he was helping
her. This was true kindness.

"I will check on your passes with Lee tomorrow. We will
try to find a convenient time for departure." Mr. Ko spoke
confidently, as though everything was arranged. "The trip
will be very long. The trains travel most slowly. You may
not have a seat inside, but may have to hang on to the outside
of the train. Many travel that way now. It would be best if
you rested up for the trip, and gave yourself enough time to
prepare carefully."

"Your words are wise. Perhaps a month would be enough.
I am feeling better every day. I think that by then the baby
and I both would be ready for travel."

"And how is the little one?" Mr. Ko looked toward the
bedroom. They could hear the baby making contented little
sounds as he stirred in his bed.

"Would you like to see? I know we won't disturb him. He
has had more visitors than the Emperor's baby." Choo stood
up laughing, and led the way into the other room.

The rest of the day was spent in repairing the windows in
the house. Most of them had been blown out by the bombs,

and there was no glass to replace them. But Lee found a roll of oiled paper stored away in one of the cupboards, and they used that.

Lee found it pleasant working with Mr. Ko. Together they cut the paper to size, and fitted it into the many small openings. The paper blocked much light, but it would serve to keep the wind out. It would be all right for the next month, but after that the days and nights would be cold. The thought of the southern trip was pleasant to Lee.

"I think that going to the South is an excellent idea," said Mr. Ko as he carefully fitted a piece of paper between the edges of wood molding.

"Yes, and that fact is probably in the minds of many, too." Lee tightened the molding to hold the paper taut.

"There is no question about that. Many will be trying to get out of the city. The flood of people is not good. Many have no place to go, but they fear the return of the Communists. They would rather take their chances in Taegu or Pusan than to stay here and live with the enemy, should they return. I don't anticipate that prospect, but I feel that anyone can live with them if he is careful." Mr. Ko set the window carefully back into its groove, and slid it open and shut to make sure that it worked properly.

"I have been thinking," said Lee slowly, "when the family is settled at the farm, I will be more free. My duties will not be so great once I know that they are safe. And they will be at Grandmother's."

"I suspect that you are thinking again of the war?"

"Yes. I am not the child that I once was. I have learned much in the last few days."

Mr. Ko looked at him for a moment. "Yes, one can see that. Your face is older. Your eyes speak of many things. When the past is not as close, you must tell me your story. Do you think that you will be able to join the army?"

"I would rather do something else." Lee looked at the old man for a moment. "I have the feeling that there are many important things that I could do, if only I knew where to begin. I will spend some time looking in Taegu when I am visiting my aunt there. I shall be going into the city every two weeks with rice and I will use part of that time to see what is available."

"If I know you, you will be finding something very soon. Ah, here I yearn for only peace and contentment, and you are already tired of the quiet. That must be the difference between youth and old age." Mr. Ko sat down and took the long bamboo pipe from his belt. He groped for the little package of tobacco, and stuffed some into the tiny brass bowl. "Perhaps some job with the Americans would be good for you. I remember that they were looking for houseboys when they came in after the Japanese were here. Many boys made a good living and learned the language while they worked. You might be able to do that when you go to Taegu."

"No," said Lee definitely. "No, I want to do something more. I want to have done something to drive the enemy out of our land. I will not rest until they are gone. I have seen some of the war. It has not been fun, or exciting, or any of the things that I once thought it would be." He stopped, and Mr. Ko waited for him to go on. "It has been terrible. I have been sick with fear and terror. Now, I am better. Now I can see a little more clearly. I think that I am ready to help."

Mr. Ko sat for a few moments puffing on his long pipe. The tip pushed its way through his sparse white beard, and he nibbled thoughtfully on it as he looked at Lee.

"I suppose that you have thought this over carefully. You have good judgment. I am sure that you will become involved whenever you find the opening you want."

IV Flight to Taegu

TWO MONTHS passed before they could leave for the South. During that time the few trains that did operate were filled with war and emergency relief supplies. But, as the American genius for organization took control, twisted tracks were rebuilt, trains were repaired, and the railroad began to run.

By constantly chasing his father's influential friends, and with Mr. Ko's help, Lee managed at last to obtain passes for Taegu. But all of the influence in the city could not get them seats on the train. There were thousands of people waiting in the station yard to board all trains going south. They waited days to get on the train. When one came in, there would be a mad rush, and then the train would puff away leaving many behind to wait for the next one. By the time the next train arrived, thousands more people had been added to the crowd of refugees.

Lee watched at the station for several days before deciding what to do. He knew that his mother could never fight her way to the train, much less to a seat. They would have to stand for many days before even getting close enough to the tracks to try to board. Furthermore, the train's schedule was not dependable. It could arrive at any time, and leave without any warning.

"So many thousands of people are going south." Lee shook his head mournfully as he told Mr. Ko what he had seen. "No one is coming north. I thought that the refugees would be returning to the city as soon as it was free. But the trains coming from the south are almost empty of Koreans. They carry only army personnel."

"It is too bad that you are not going the other way. You would be able to ride in comfort." Mr. Ko chuckled without any humor.

"Yes. That would be ideal." Lee shook his head. Then he stared at Mr. Ko. "Of course! That is just it! We are thinking of the wrong direction. We must go north!"

"Oh, my dear child, the strain has been too much for you. Are you saying that you want to go north instead of south?" The old man looked quizzically at Lee who was laughing at the simplicity of the idea that had struck him.

"No, no. What I mean is, why shouldn't we leave the city, go south a few miles on foot, and then board the train coming to Seoul. We will stay on the train until it goes back down south again." Lee laughed triumphantly. "Of course we will need some money. I am sure that such an idea is against the rules. There will be much permission to gain. The best way of doing that is with money to give to the officials and the train men."

"I must admit that the idea has a great deal of merit," Mr. Ko agreed. "I can help you with the papers that will enable you to cross the Han River and return to the city. I have no idea how I shall explain to the officials why you and your family want to leave the city on foot, return a few hours later by train, and then leave immediately again to go to Taegu." He shook his head, "Officials are difficult to convince of the most obvious things. Something as complicated as this will probably leave them hopelessly confused." He stood up. "But we shall try. I will see what I can do as far as the necessary money goes, too. I may be able to raise a little."

"And I will go to all my father's friends. There are still many left in the city. I think that they will be able to help." Lee looked thoughtful. "Of course it is not a good thing to ask one's friends for money. But there is no other way, is there?"

"I am afraid not. You will shock a good many of those venerable men, but one or two may just do something for you. Right now it is worth trying."

"Right now, anything is worth trying that gets us out of the city." Lee took out a piece of paper and pencil. "I am going to list all of the men who might help. Tomorrow I will find them, and I will ask them for money one by one."

"Good. I will do my best for you tomorrow, too. We will meet back here and see what success we have had."

From early morning to late afternoon, Lee sought out his father's friends. He went to their homes, to their offices recently reopened in the buildings left standing. He spotted some of them on the streets, and found some in the various tearooms around Seoul. Before each he swallowed his shame, and came right to the point. He asked them for money for the trip south. Some of the men were appalled at his impolite-

ness, and they turned away from him in anger. Some pro-
ceeded to lecture him on the collapse of his morals that allowed him to go begging in the streets. But some listened
sympathetically to his reasons, and they gave as much as they
could.

When Lee arrived home late that afternoon, he counted
the money, and was overjoyed to find that he had more than
enough for the trip. As money was worth so little, "enough"
money made a huge bundle. He counted it into small packets,
and tied each with string. In this way, he could use them as
needed, knowing how much he was giving out for each favor.

He had just finished counting out the money and tying it
up when Mr. Ko came noisily in. Lee could see by his face
that the old man was very angry.

"Such donkeys. I have never seen so much delay and inso-
lence." He stomped to a chair and sat down. "But, in spite of
all their ignorance, I managed to get what we wanted." He
reached into his pocket and pulled out a sheaf of papers. "The
Lee family may leave Seoul on foot, return on the train, and
leave the city on the train within this time period." The time
was a week away, Lee saw, and he felt that the plans were
going well.

"Now we must get food and all the things we wish to carry
ready. I will tell my mother. She will be able to take care of

that." Lee jumped up and called to her. Choo came hurrying out of the kitchen where she had been sitting with some of the neighbors.

"What is it? Has anything happened?" she looked worriedly from one to the other. Lee told her what had taken place, and how much time they had before they must leave. As he spoke, he could see Choo making a mental list of things that they would need. She nodded quickly, listening to the details.

"I think that we can be ready in that time. There is much to be done. We will need a great quantity of food for such a long journey. I think enough for a week would not be too much, don't you, Mr. Ko?"

"In my opinion, that would scarcely be enough. I know your generous heart. You will see much suffering on the way. I would take more so that you may do all you can to help those who have nothing."

"Your wisdom makes me humble. I had not thought of that. Of course, we shall take as much as we can carry."

"Now," Mr. Ko said, "I have arranged for a cart to carry you part of the way to Suwon. It will take many hours to get there, and there is no way of knowing when the train will be going through. We will have to stay at the station until we can board."

"You say 'We'," Lee said. "Do you mean that you are going with us?"

"I will go to Suwon and back. It will make me feel better knowing that you are off safely. Further, you will need someone to help you take the things. An extra pair of hands will be of help." Mr. Ko looked a little self-consciously at them. "It is a long way to go. We will have to travel for two days. If we ride in the cart, we will not be too tired. But there will be more than enough for us to do with the baby. Yes, I think that it is best this way."

"You are very kind," Choo said softly. "I hope that one day we may be able to repay you for all you have done."

"Nonsense. You can best repay me by going south and being safe. That is what I want you to do. When you are safe, then we will all breathe a little better."

And so it was arranged. The days passed quickly, and on the appointed morning a small farmer's cart pulled by a tired old bullock creaked down the alley to the Lee's house. Sitting on the seat was a dusty man in farmer's dress of brown pants and shirt, with a wide straw hat on his head. He smiled pleasantly at them, his face crinkling into many little lines. Climbing down, he helped them load the cart, putting the bedding into one corner so that it made a comfortable place for Choo to recline with the child. Mr. Ko was the last one out of the house, and he hung the key in the familiar place. Pulling his full white coat around him, he climbed awkwardly up into the seat beside the driver.

Choo and Lee looked back at the house. It stood dark and alone in its corner of the alley. The windows were shuttered under the low, tiled roof, and it seemed terribly empty. They looked at each other as the cart wheeled into the street, and the house was lost from sight. Both were thinking the same thoughts. When would they see it again? It would never be the same. The river had changed its course by too much.

Choo looked into Lee's face as the cart bumped noisily over the rutted street. She saw the deep hollows under his eyes, the way his cheekbones stood out sharply. She saw the look of age that had crept almost imperceptibly over his face in the last few months. She saw, then closed her eyes. In one arm she held her baby close to her. With her other hand she groped for Lee's, and held it tightly. He watched her face and realized that they had never been more close. In those few seconds she had known, somehow, what he had done, who he was. Her dry hand in his told him without words that she understood. And he knew that to understand was to forgive. For the first time in many weeks he felt free. He, too, closed his eyes, and leaned against the thick roll of bedding, feeling her warmth nearby.

Their plan worked. They had to stand as they rode back to Seoul, as all the seats were filled with soldiers and army gear. Mr. Ko maneuvered them to a spot on the platform, and they huddled there in the cold. The trip was short, lasting less than two hours, before the train chugged into the Seoul station. Even over the noise of the engine, they could hear the roar of the crowd of refugees that waited to board. The soldiers jumped out of their seats, and filed off, lining up in disorderly rows on the platform. It took time for the men to march out to the waiting trucks, to change engines and reverse the seats, in that time the refugees could not board. Mr. Ko led the Lees to a seat at the back of a car, and he helped them to arrange their bundles.

"Remember, do not leave anything under this front seat. Someone could reach under and take your things. Keep most of it in your laps." He put the food under the window. "If you get chilly, wrap the blankets around you. The trip will be long, and the wind is cold. There is no heat." He and Lee arranged a quilt around Choo and the baby. Just then a storm of refugees swept toward the train. The shouts around them were deafening. Mr. Ko looked up. "I must go, or I will end in Pusan." His quick eyes scanned them, then, reassured, he smiled his farewell, and began pushing his way toward the door. He disappeared in the mob, and a few minutes later they saw him on the platform being buffeted about by the pushing refugees. In moments he was swallowed up.

The train was full, and still the people came. There was not an inch of standing space left in the aisle, but hundreds were crowding toward the platform to board. Lee could see the people fighting for a place to hang on outside. From the sounds overhead, many were crowded together on the roof, too. How lucky they had been to get on the way they had. Choo could never have gotten through this. He tried to see who the people were in the train, but even the arms of his seat were filled, and all he could see were the backs of the men who sat there. The din was terrific, and a mixed odor of onions and sweat hung like a pall over the car. Some men were smoking, and the acrid smell of burning tobacco was almost pleasant in comparison.

Steam hissed, and the whistle began to blow the warning that the train was ready to start. Still the battle raged for a handhold on the sides of the train. The cars gave a jolt, and very slowly began to move. Lee tried to see out the window, but it had steamed up, and he could only hear the cries of those left on the platform as they moved out of the way of the great grinding wheels. Faster, faster the train began to move, and while Lee could not see the platform, he could hear the voices. He could hear the cries of desperation, and he reached across his brother to wipe the steam away from the window. But the train had already left the platform behind, and they were rolling into the train yard. This time the soldiers did not check the papers at the Han River. It would have been an impossible task. The train stopped there for a few minutes, and Lee saw the Han River below. How different it looked now that winter was coming. It had shrunk to almost the size of a stream. He remembered the night when the family had tried to escape the city, and the river was swollen with the spring rains until it surged like a living thing. He could see, too, the twisted girders of the old bridge, and the blasted concrete pillars. The girders were like gnarled fingers of a giant hand that clutched at the cold, gray autumn sky.

Choo sat quietly in the corner by the window. She had not seen anything like this before and she was confused. The edge of desperation that was in the people soon found its way into her and she trembled, sitting there. Lee reached forward and pulled the quilt higher around her shoulders. She shook her head, "It is not a chill from outside me, it is from within." Her eyes moved up to the mass of people pressed together in the aisle. Then she saw something.

"Lee," her voice was quiet. He turned and looked behind. A short distance down the aisle a young woman stood holding on to the edge of a seat as she swayed with the motion of the train. On her back she carried a baby in a sling. Her eyes were wide with fear. Lee stood up and pushed towards her. "There is a seat here for you," he shouted. She did not understand. Her fear was too great. Lee took her arm firmly and pulled her behind him as he made his way back to his family. He settled the girl in his seat, and put a quilt around her. She held the baby on her lap. It was sleeping. All the noise and smell of the train had not kept it awake.

"What is your name?" Choo asked the girl.

"Pahk Yung Ja," the girl said. "My husband is in the army. I am going to his people in Pusan." She spoke quickly, her face flushed with shyness. Choo smiled at her, and reached into her bundle. She came up with a package of rice cakes, and handed them to the girl. "You have probably not been able to eat, waiting for the train. Here. Eat now." Choo reached down again, and brought out more.

"I haven't eaten since yesterday." The girl ate quickly, smiling at them as they began to eat.

"Mr. Ko was right." Choo smiled at the girl. "Our friend told us to bring much food. I'm glad we can share with you."

As they talked, the baby awoke. The girl looked a little startled. "Oh, I think he is hungry." Her cheeks flamed.

"You must feed him."

The girl looked at the men standing near. Choo understood, and stood up heavily. She bent over the young mother, and pulled the quilt up around the girl to shield her from the curious eyes. "There, I understand how hard it is when you are young. I think you can manage it now." When the child had finished, the girl thanked her, and they settled back to rest.

Hour after hour the train headed south. There were stops at one or two stations, but no one seemed to get off. Many tried to board, but with little success. Night came quickly, and the darkness made rest easier. Here and there in the crowded train there were hushed voices and the glow of cigarettes. Lee leaned against the arm of his mother's seat trying to stay awake. His head bobbed up and down as sleep tried to claim him. Dimly, he heard the train grind to a halt, and the people began to stir with much commotion. He tugged at the man next to him.

"Where?" he asked sleepily.

"Taegu," the man answered.

Lee reached over and shook his mother and told her. They

began gathering their bundles about them. The girl, Yung Ja, helped them get things together. She stood up, being careful not to wake her baby, and took the quilt from her shoulders to fold it.

"No," Choo said firmly, "you will need that. We have others." She reached over and draped it around the girl's shoulders again.

"Thank you, Mother. You are very kind."

"I am sorry we have to say good-by so soon after meeting. I hope that things work out well for you. If you are ever in Seoul after this war business is over, come and see us. Be sure and bring the baby and your husband. We will be glad to welcome you." Choo told the address, and with more good-bys, they pushed their way through the thinning crowd to the train steps.

They edged their way carefully through the people until they came to a free corner of the gray stone station.

"I think that we should stay here for the night. It will be impossible to get any transportation at this hour." Lee dropped his bundles, and made cushions for Choo to sit on. The air was cold, but not as bad as near Seoul. They would have to stay outdoors for the night, but if they crowded together, they would be warm enough. Lee glanced over the hundreds of people who were planning to do the same. They had settled down, some around little fires, some just curling up in blankets, if they had them, to spend the night.

"Come close, my children. We will try to stay warm until morning." Choo drew the two boys to her, and cradled the baby close to her breast. They pulled the warm quilts around, tucking in all the loose edges. It was not long before they had drifted off to sleep.

The morning was gray and cold. A damp wind pushed wisps of fog before it as the watery yellow sun tried to break through the clouds. Lee opened his eyes, and guessed that it must be about six o'clock. Only a few of the families had begun to stir. He got up carefully, and stepping over the many prostrate forms, made his way to the street.

A few farmers and their carts were moving toward the market place which was in the center of Taegu. The cart wheels creaked and groaned as they were pulled along by the men bent double by the weight. Some of them carried huge loads of produce on their backs in A frames, so-called because they were wooden carriers shaped like inverted A's. All moved slowly. They had left their farms early, Lee knew, so that they could get a favorable spot in the square. The late-comers would have the fringe areas, and they would not sell all their vegetables before the sun began to wilt them.

Among the things being brought in, Lee could see the huge

cabbages that had been so long absent from Seoul. Their long feathery leaves had been one of the staples of his family's diet before the war. He saw the bags of grain and the many other vegetables, and he eagerly followed the carts into the heart of the city.

It had been more than three years since he had visited here. While Taegu seemed almost as big as Seoul, the buildings were not as tall, nor as grand as in the capital. As he walked, it seemed to Lee that the damage from the war was not as great as in the North.

Perhaps, he thought, it is because there are so many American army camps near here. He passed two on his way into the city. They were just beginning to stir into life, and he stopped to watch for a few minutes. He saw lights flashing on in the rows of concrete barracks, and heard rough voices speaking in the strange tongue. A scratchy record blared over the area from concealed speakers. The sudden music was startling in the hushed streets.

As Lee came closer to the central square of Taegu, the voices around him grew more strident, the carts rattled furiously over the cobbled streets. He drank in the sight and sounds. This was so like the Korea he had known before the war that he could almost imagine the war had never happened. The dusty farmers shouting the virtues of their produce, the old women huddled near the curb before smoking charcoal fires in little brass stoves cooking bean cakes for the workers, the early housewives examining the wares cautiously or haggling over their choice noisily — all this was the Korea that Lee knew. His eyes sparkled hungrily as the smoke from nearby fires wafted the smells of cooking food to him.

Moving between the carts to one of the old women, he had her cook and wrap enough bean and rice cakes for his family. Hurrying back toward the station, he darted through the traffic that was now charging through the narrow streets. Army trucks and jeeps beeped furiously at him as he skipped across the streets.

At the station he picked his way through the crowds to his family. They had folded and packed all the blankets, and were looking around anxiously for him. Choo saw him coming and waved. "I thought that you would never get back," she called. They ate the food he had brought, and asked many questions about the city. He told what he had seen, and said, "I think that we will have to walk to the farm. I saw nothing that we could hire to take us. Most of the farmers are pulling their own wagons, they don't have many bullocks."

"Then we shall have to walk. It is not too far. I think that the trip will take no more than four hours. If we start now, we will get there by noon." Choo looked at them all to see if this was agreeable. Lee nodded and stooped to hoist the heaviest bundle to his shoulders. He helped Yung Sin load, and then they were ready.

They had to stop for frequent rests along the road, but their pace was good. The morning had brightened, and the sunshine was warm as noon approached. They passed few people, for the traffic almost stopped after the farmers trooped into town. It would not begin again until they were ready to return at the end of their selling day.

As they walked, Choo kept pointing out spots that were reminders of her childhood before she had married and gone to Seoul to live.

"And over there, my sons, is where your father first saw me. I was with my family, and it was one of those beautiful days in May. We had all dressed in our finest clothes because the time had come to celebrate the Festival of the Swings. We had a wonderful swing in that old oak tree." She pointed to a small grassy knoll that was off to their right. An ancient tree stood there, its gnarled branches looking strong enough to hold a dozen swings. Behind the tree the land dropped to the terraced rice paddies that stretched away in tailored rusty brown squares.

"It was early evening before the festival was really exciting. A full moon had just risen. There were many girls from the farms all around. I knew that your father was to be there. My family had invited him down to catch a glimpse of me. Of course, it was forbidden for us to exchange words, as that couldn't happen until after the wedding. Our families had arranged everything. We could only obey." Choo stopped for a moment by the side of the road. "When I saw him, I was delighted with my parent's choice." She walked on remembering a moon-drenched night so many years ago when she had fallen in love. "I remember that the mist was rising, and it made everything seem so unreal. I was swinging, and my ribbons . . . oh, you should have seen how they streamed out behind me as I swung higher and higher. It seemed as though everyone was there watching, and we all felt very wonderful. When I had finished swinging, I saw him. My mother had described him a dozen times and I knew him right away. I felt so giddy, I was a little dizzy from the swings, and my cheeks were flushed. I stood there and looked at him for a long moment, and then I went back to my family.

They told me that I was a very bold girl because they had seen me staring at him so hard." Choo laughed. "I suppose it was not delicate. But I wanted at least to see the man I was going to marry."

The two boys laughed with her, and her good humor made the trip go quickly. It was a little after noon when they spotted the familiar farmhouse nestled at the foot of a low hill. The sunlight touched the thatched straw roof with golden fingers, and a welcome curl of smoke drifted up from the chimney.

Lee moved ahead to rouse Grandmother. He could not run as his bundles were so heavy that he would have lost balance and fallen. He moved awkwardly, and when he was within a few yards of the front gate, he shouted, "Grandmother, Grandmother . . ."

The door ahead opened, and a tiny, gray-haired woman stepped over the high threshold. She squinted against the sun, and, recognizing Lee, she cackled in joy calling him by his old name.

"Yung Chang, Yung Chang, such a surprise!" She hurried forward to embrace him, and saw the others just turning in at the gate. She hurried to her daughter with noisy delight. They went into the house all talking at once. After they had put the baby to bed, and found a room for all their things, she herded them off to the kitchen to exchange all the news and eat.

It was late afternoon before they were caught up. They had eaten a huge lunch, and were feeling better than at any time for many days. A new calm was invading Lee. How good it was to know peace, and to be secure. He looked out into the quickly darkening valley. There was not a sound beyond the thick windows. There was no traffic rushing back and forth, there were no guns monotonously thumping. He had almost forgotten what silence could be like.

He called Yung Sin, and together they settled the bedding, putting Choo's things near Grandmother's room. The boys shared the other bedroom.

"Lee, we are so lucky to be here. There are many who have no place to go. They have to stay in the city."

"Yes, we are lucky. It is good for Grandmother too. Now she won't have to depend on the neighborhood men to help her on the farm." Lee snuggled down under the covers. It was warm and comfortable here, but again the thought of all those others came to his mind. He must be able to help them, to help Korea. That was what he wanted to do . . . It was what he had to do if he were really to be a man. He would find a way. Now that the family was safe, he was free to find a way to help. The idea persisted like a little hammer beating in his drowsy brain.

V Search for Adventure

AT THE farm, Lee found himself growing strong and sure again. The doubts that had crowded into his mind in Seoul now were draining away. The fight to live had been so bitter in the city that it had begun to seem as though he would spend his entire life struggling just for enough to eat, and never quite succeeding. The dust, the terror, the noise of the city had seeped into his mind and dimmed all youthful hopes for the future until he felt gray and old.

The late autumn country sun flooded away all his fear and

doubt and washed his mind clean of the horror he had seen. The scars were still there — often he was torn out of sleep by grotesque dreams that paralyzed him with terror. But even they were beginning to yield to the calm new life.

He found the work hard, but good. There was much to be done. The rice paddies had to be plowed, and he soon grew adept at guiding the plow while the old bullock pulled slowly, patiently.

He shared the plowing with his brother, and together they finished in time to plant the winter barley in the fields beside the house. Soon the "winter clothes," as the snow was called, would come to cover their planting, keeping the seed warm.

Their next task was to gather enough wood for the winter. Every day he and Yung Sin traveled out over the fields stacking wood into their A frames. When they had piled enough of the brush, they went to the slopes of the distant hills for heavier logs. They would cut with their sharp axes until there was one load, then one or the other would carry the A frame strapped over his shoulders, back to the farm.

For the first weeks Lee and his brother were so tired from this unaccustomed labor that they would eat their evening meal and go right to bed, sleeping until morning. But as their bodies became hard, they were soon able to stay up and talk, or play chess. Often, too, they would all sit around the fire in the kitchen and sing the plaintive folk songs of the country people. Grandmother would lead in her quavering, hoarse voice, singing the first line, and then all would join singing the rest with her. They would sing the quick joyous songs gustily, stamping their feet to the beat. Then, in contrast, the sad songs were sung softly. The words of the gentle ballads were close to them, and had a personal meaning for each. Grandmother would hum the melody, marking the rhythm with her gnarled hand. They would sit gazing into the fire, as though the words were there. After a while, another song would begin almost by itself.

Of all the songs they sang, there was one that Lee liked particularly well. It was a tender ballad of lost love, and parting. The words called up a nameless sadness in him. He would find the words running through his mind as he worked, and he would begin to sing:

> Oh, my loved one. Oh, my loved one,
> Why must we part?
> Green hill, pine trees,
> Nevermore to see you there.

> Farewell. A road of danger is ahead.
> This is our parting,
> Without the promise to meet again . . .

Without the promise to meet again. So simple, and yet so full of meaning. He would lean on his hoe looking off to the distant mountains rising in the north. The far peaks were shrouded in soft mist, and the bare winter-ready slopes seemed to be calling to him, softly . . . softly.

These were feelings that he could share with no one. He knew that one day destiny would call him to those northern mountains, and he knew that he must prepare. In a few more weeks the farm work would be done outside. Only the mending of harness, the sharpening of tools and the many little jobs that had to be done on a farm in winter would remain. He would not really be needed. That would be the time to go into the city to answer the call to adventure that rang so loudly in his mind.

Taegu was becoming more familiar to him. Every ten days or so he would take the farm's produce in to the market place, and when he had sold it all, he would take an hour or two to walk through the streets, to talk with the other boys and the farmers. More and more he would drift to the gates of the American army companies to peer at the swarming activity within. He could only get as far as the gates without a pass. The American sentries would allow him to stand there and watch, but if the guard was Korean, he would be chased away.

On one of his visits to the city, Lee found several books on learning English. He had been searching the stalls for them. He had had three years of English in school, but like many, he had not seen the need of a foreign language, and so did not pay much attention to the instructor. He had dutifully learned many of the basic rules, how to speak simple sentences, but his pronunciation was poor. With his new books, he spent many hours, night after night, learning how to put the complicated language together. His mother watched him studying by the light of the oil lamp, and a vague fear began to stir inside of her. She could not sense his purpose, but she could tell that he had one, and that it was a threat to the way they were living. She would often comment on her "scholar son," but Lee would only smile without explaining beyond saying, "Oh, it is just good to know another language." Then he would return to his books.

As he studied, he found that he remembered a good deal more than he had originally supposed. He slowly built his reading and writing vocabulary, but he could only imagine the sounds of the words. Even in school, the master's pronunciation had been very poor. Many words now, had to be guessed at. He realized that he would have to practice speaking, but there seemed to be no way to do this. To practice, he would have to talk to Americans. To talk to Americans, he would have to know how to speak. The circle depressed him.

He began to grow restless on the farm. More and more he spent his days looking forward to the trips to the city. For a few hours he could plunge into the activity of the market place, and hope that something would happen to get him into the action up north.

One day, a messenger came to the farmhouse. Lee ran in from the fields to see what had happened. They were all over-joyed to find that the messenger came from Aunt, who had hidden them and Mr. Lee the night the Communists had first taken Seoul. She had come to her house in Taegu city that she had told them about before. Her immediate need was food, the messenger told them. Grandmother told Lee to prepare sacks of grain and other supplies to take to Taegu in the morning. Choo told him that he might stay overnight, if he wished, to be sure that Aunt was settled. Lee was delighted. He would have time to see more of the city, and he could at last share his plans with someone who would understand and help.

Weighted down by the supplies that were going to Aunt, Lee hurried to the city the next morning even before the sun had risen. He pushed himself so that the trip would go fast. When he finally turned into her street, sweat was spilling down his face, and his legs were weak with exhaustion. He staggered up to the address the messenger had given, and pounded hard on the door. It was swept open in a moment, and he recognized the familiar face.

"Aunt!" he cried, smiling broadly.

"Aye-ooo, is it really you?" She looked at him in disbelief, then tried to embrace him, but could not with all that he was carrying.

"Come take those things off . . . Are they for me?" She clasped her hands and rolled her eyes upward when he nodded yes. "Oh, how good. It will be so good to eat again. And so much you have brought me. But, look." She clutched the front of her dress, "Look, I am almost nothing. I have lost so much weight." She helped him unfasten the A frame harness, and lower the bundles to the floor. Lee looked around the house. It was very nice, and was partly furnished with tables and chairs in the Western style.

"This is the first time I have seen a Korean house furnished this way," he said.

"My second husband liked these things. He brought them from Japan. I have not been here since he died. They are comfortable once you are used to them. It seems strange to sit that high above the floor at first." She moved about the room with much vigor. And then, as she remembered his long trip, she pushed him toward a chair saying, "Sit down. You must be exhausted. How long can you stay?"

"I do not have to return until tomorrow. I was told to make sure that you were comfortable, and then I could return home." He grinned at her.

"Well, this food was all that I really needed. Everything must be good at the farm, eh?"

"Yes. The crop was heavy this year. We have much."

"Good. But a word from the gods. Don't trade it all. Save some for next year. They say that the crop will be small then. That means that the price will go up like spring flood water." She hurried to the kitchen to fix them some of the new rice. "All I have from my trip is a little kim-chi. I brought a jar with me on the train. It will taste good with the rice." As she spoke, she poked into a red clay jar, and brought out a few spoonfuls of pickled cabbage and fish. "My kim-chi is fine, but when you have nothing else to go with it, you soon find its virtues dwindling." She put on the water for rice and for tea, and began to get out dishes. "You have not seen the rest of the house. Take a look while I work here. Then we will put away all the lovely supplies you brought."

Lee went back into the little sitting room, and then into the rooms along the hall. One was fixed up much like his father's study had been in Seoul but there were many more books. They lined one wall from ceiling to floor. He went to them looking at the titles avidly. Lee was surprised to find that a good many of them were in English. It was like finding a hidden treasure. He could learn much from these. Aunt would let him borrow them, and in the reading he would see how the many words he had been learning were put together into sentences.

Most of the furniture in the other rooms was in the Western style. He was awed by the beautiful rugs on the floor, and the silken coverings on the bed in the room that he guessed was Aunt's. There were even billowing white curtains at the open windows. He hurried back to the kitchen.

"It is all so fine. I have seen nothing like it before."

"Yes. He liked the Western way of doing things. His business took him often to Japan, and there he saw many of these things for the first time. He did well in business, and could afford to have furniture shipped to our home here. Yes, he did very well, but he died at thirty-five." She shook her head. "Such a waste," she said, stirring the pots on the low stove. The kitchen was Korean in total disregard of the rest of the house. Lee felt more comfortable here. He liked the low iron stove that radiated warmth through the whole house on cold days, the brown walls, and the hard-packed earth floor. These were as familiar to him as were the big rusty-red clay water and kim-chi jars that stood in the corner.

He carried the brass spoons and bowls that shone like gold

from Aunt's scouring, into the warm room next to the kitchen. There he set them on a low black table.

"Aunt, perhaps I can bring you firewood from the country. You will find that a hard thing to get here. As far as can be seen, even the smallest twig is gone." He came into the kitchen again. "Probably the price is way up on that."

"I have no problem there. The shed in back is piled high with logs. We stocked up well before the war, and no one has been here to use the supplies since."

"That will save many trips, then," Lee said a little ruefully. "I thought that you would be needing much from the farm."

"Only food for the time being." Aunt looked at him, and seeing his regret that he would not be able to come to see her as often as he had thought, she said, "Of course there is another consideration."

"What is that," Lee asked eagerly.

"I hardly dare mention it to you without speaking to your mother first." She looked thoughtfully out of the window for a moment. Lee waited impatiently for her to tell him what was in her mind.

"You know," she began slowly, "it is very difficult for a woman to be alone in the city. Things are rapidly getting worse in Taegu with the flood of refugees that have been pouring in. The water supply is gone from all of the houses, and one has to go to the well with that jar to get a little. That is a long walk. Then I have to pay someone strong enough to carry the jar back for me after standing in line often for hours to get it filled. But that is only one item." She stirred her tea slowly. "I could bring in a little income if I could use this house to advantage. Look at all those empty rooms. How many people living in the streets would welcome the chance to use them?"

"You could rent them out, couldn't you? That would bring in a fine amount. If the city is as full as you say, and with more people coming every day, you could do very well." Lee caught some of her thought. "Of course, it wouldn't do for a woman living alone to have strangers in the house." He shook his head watching her from the corner of his eye.

"That is what I am thinking." She smiled a little. He saw, and grinned. That started them, and they laughed loudly. It was many minutes before Aunt could speak.

"How carefully we play with our idea. We are both thinking the same thing, but we are diplomatically avoiding the words." She became serious then. "I would like to have you stay here, but the final decision will rest with your mother. If you are needed at the farm, then that will decide for us."

"I will speak to her on my return. I am sure that she will agree. Our work for the winter is almost done. All that is left is easy. My brother and they can finish. I want to live here very much."

"Yes, yes, I think you do. But I do not flatter myself that I am the whole cause of your desire. There is something else in your mind. I am thinking of our little talk in Seoul." She was indeed shrewd, Lee thought.

"I have been thinking of coming into the city for many weeks now. I believe that I can safely leave the family and try to become part of the war. How, I don't know yet. But I will find a way."

"Yes, I am sure you will. Perhaps after I am a little more settled I will be able to help you. I know many people. Among them there must be one who can help you get involved." She stood up, gathering the dishes. "Now, go and look at the books in the other room. If you do come here, you will be using them. Learning does not stop or start with school." He smiled his thanks at her and went in to the books. They were different from any that he had seen before. Big, with colorful dust jackets, they made the small paper-bound Korean books seem poor indeed by comparison. He opened a few at random, and was delighted that he could read many of the words.

"You have found something?" Aunt came into the room.

"Yes. Many things are here that will help me. I have been

trying to learn the English language. But now I need some-one to speak to in English. That will be the difficult job."

"Yes. You know that most of the soldiers are not permitted to visit the Korean houses. It is a silly rule, but one that is strictly enforced. They have a curfew at night, and no one may be on the streets after the curfew signal has sounded."

"What time is that?"

"Nine o'clock."

"I will have to be careful not to be out at that time if I come here to live."

"Well, I suppose that there is good reason for it, but I can't see the sense. That is when the evening is just beginning. This rule kills all chance of social life. I had thought, too, that now would be a good chance to get to know the Ameri-cans. We have heard so much about them, and we have seen them about so often that it would seem wise to permit us to mingle." She sighed. "Ah, well. War is a funny business."

"How do you think I can get to see someone who might help me? I have thought of nothing, yet," Lee said.

"It would seem to me that you might wait for an opportu-nity. There is very little you can do in direct action. Just wait and see what happens. Something will turn up, it always does when you want it to very badly."

When Lee was in bed later, he kept hoping that something

would turn up soon. He didn't want to spend the rest of the
war just waiting. That would be unbearable.

The next day Lee said good-by to Aunt, and promised to
come soon again, and, he hoped that when he did it would be
with good news. He felt certain that his mother would ap-
prove of their plans. As he walked through the streets, he began to whistle to himself. Ahead he saw the entrance to an
army company. It was very busy this morning. Many trucks
and jeeps were pulling in and out at the entrance, and Lee
saw that the Korean sentry was dashing about in a fury of
activity.

Lee stopped across the street to watch for a while. If he
could only get in there and see somebody. Where he would
go, or who he might see, he couldn't guess. But he was certain
that there was some way. All he had to do was to find it. He
nodded his head. He would find a way.

He headed toward home reluctantly. The road to the farm
was dull, with little traffic. Only an occasional army truck
roared past him, and left a billowing cloud of dust in its wake.
He plodded on wearily, lost in his thoughts. A raucous beep-
ing almost directly behind him shattered his revery, and he
jumped to the side of the road apprehensively.

"Want a ride?" An American soldier leaned out of the
truck window and opened the door near Lee. Without hesita-

tion, Lee jumped up to the high seat, and smiled happily at the driver. The truck started with a jolt, and the roaring engine noise frightened him at first.

"How far are you going?" the driver shouted.

Lee understood the "how far" and tried to answer, but the words would not come. He held up eight fingers. "That much," he shouted back over the noise. The driver seemed to understand, and nodded at him. As the truck jounced over the rutted dirt road the driver began to sing lustily, interrupting himself to make comments on the condition of Korean roads, and various other facets of life in the Orient.

"I've never seen anything like it before in all my life." The driver shook his head. "Wild country you live in." Lee nodded happily, not understanding.

It did not take long to get to the farm. Lee tugged at the man's sleeve and pointed to the farmhouse ahead. "There. I live." The truck slowed to a quick halt, and Lee hopped down. He smiled his thanks, and waved as the truck rolled off down the road.

Such an experience! He had been jolted to the core, and his legs felt wobbly. They must be strong people to survive truck rides such as that. It was worse than any wagon. He went up to the house, and saw his family peeping through the windows. They were full of questions as to how he had gotten a ride in such a noisy monster. He told them what had happened, and how his trip had gone.

"Then everything seems to be all right in the city?" Choo asked.

"Yes," Lee replied. "Aunt is fine, although she is much thinner. She welcomed the food. I think that it is very hard for her living there alone. She needs money, too." He told them about Aunt's house, and how it could make money if she had someone there to live with her so that she could have guests and would not be alone. Carefully he worked up to his going there and taking care of things. Choo was undecided about such a move, but Grandmother thought it a good idea.

"We will see him less often, but he can help her very much. She should not be alone in the city. I would worry about her. And Lee will come often to take the produce to market."

"I know, but I don't like the idea," Choo said reluctantly.

"I am sure that it will be all right. He is a boy of good sense . . ."

"Of course. But he is still young, and . . . oh, I suppose it will be satisfactory for a while, anyway."

Those were the words he had been waiting to hear. He smiled joyously, and hugged Choo until she gasped.

It was agreed that Lee would leave the next time he went

to market. He could take the produce in, and return the money when he came out to take the next load ten days later. He finished all of the work he could in the remaining time, and studied feverishly at night, cramming as many words as possible into his head. As he worked in the day, he would repeat sentences that he had learned the night before. Often his brother would find him in the fields muttering in the foreign language, "Good morning, Sir. How are you today." Lee enunciated the words carefully, and it is true that the effect was strange. Yung Sin would laugh loudly, and Lee would scowl back at him. "Go away, little idiot. You are too young to know the ways of knowledge. You laugh in your ignorance, but I learn to eliminate mine." He would begin to work furiously, until Yung Sin left him in peace. And then he would begin practicing again.

The days dragged. He counted almost every minute as time moved with the sun across the sky. With relief he saw Grandmother begin to prepare the market goods. He did not need much time to wrap up his few clothes. His books took little room. When the day finally came, he awoke before anyone else. They heard him moving about, and Choo hurried out to fix his breakfast. He ate quickly, still impatient to be gone. She kept slowing him down, making him chew his food carefully, and generally calming him. He realized that she was concerned and that she would miss him when he was gone, and so he stilled his impatience.

When the sun had been up for more than two hours, there was finally nothing more to detain him, and he gathered his things together.

"Do you have everything?" Choo asked softly.

"Yes, I think so." He moved to the door, saying good-by to them.

"Remember, in ten days you will return. I will worry if I don't see you." Choo patted his shoulder. "Take good care of yourself." He hugged her with his free arm, and went through the opening. At the curve in the road, he turned and waved to the little group that stood together in the front yard.

It did not take Lee long to become used to his new home. The life was exciting after the quiet farm. Many nights there would be visits from Aunt's friends from the North, and they would always bring the war news. Lee was happy when they heard that the Communists were driven far north and the war seemed to be almost over. Now the country would be free and they would be able to go to Seoul to begin their lives again.

He would often talk over his future with Aunt, telling her

of his plans to go back to school, and to get a good job that would make his future secure. Their evenings would pass quickly as their plans began to be more than just talk. They mapped out his schooling and his choice of profession as though planning a careful war campaign. He would re-enter the middle school, finish high school, and then go on to the university. He would finish his training for the profession that seemed to draw him the most, engineering.

Lee spent many hours poring over the books in Aunt's library, especially the English ones. They had secrets in them that he had to unravel. The language was still difficult, but it was becoming more and more understandable. He worked with his dictionary, saying the words out loud. The sense became more and more evident, and he began to read more smoothly. The conquest of these words was like a physical triumph for him. He felt the thrill of winning his way over the obstacle course of a barely familiar language, and daily he grew more confident of his ability to learn to speak the new tongue quickly.

Now the thing to do was to use what he had learned. He found it easy to talk to GIs on the streets of Taegu. They were always asking for directions to this place or that, and he was able to make himself understood.

Often in his wanderings about the city, he would find himself in front of the American army company he had first seen. For long minutes he would stare through the gates. Trucks were always roaring in and out of the entrance, there were many men hurrying here and there within the compound. His curiosity drew him closer.

The soldiers seemed always to know what they were doing, and where they were going. It was no wonder that they were winning the war so quickly, he thought as he turned to go home.

One day a knock came at the door, and Aunt let two men in. They had just come from the North, and they were full of the war news. For a long time they talked about a new threat that was breaking over Korea. The Chinese were entering the war, and were sending hordes of men against the UN forces. Slowly the UN armies were being forced back through North Korea to the South. It was becoming more and more certain that the city of Seoul would fall again to the enemy. Lee listened to this new tale, and his eyes grew wide.

"Is there no way to stop them?" he asked.

"It would seem not," the older of the two men answered. "They have so many that it is like trying to stop a tidal wave. They have prepared the way with many advance spies, so that they know just where the southern fortifications are."

"Why don't we have spies that we can use against them?

That would help us to destroy them before they came too far south."

"We do have a few in that area. But they are hard to get, and the work is very dangerous. We need people who know the places well, and could find out information without being caught . . . That is not as easy as it seems."

"That is the kind of work that I want to do. I do not want to go with the army. I want to do something by myself." The excitement was shining out of Lee's eyes.

"Well, I have known of many that have gone north. But I am not sure that you would want to travel that far with no food, no place to sleep, nothing. You must watch every word that you say. No, it is the job of experts, of men who have had much experience in these things. They are hard to find."

"You don't know how stubborn my nephew is," said Aunt, smiling. "He has been thinking of something like this for a long time. I doubt if you will be able to change his mind so quickly." She went to the kitchen to get a jug of rice wine for her guests.

"I would like to talk to you more if you are seriously interested. We do not turn anyone down without a hearing." The man lit his pipe slowly. Both of the men were watching Lee closely, and he noticed this. It was only after they had gone to their rooms that his aunt told him why they had come.

"I had talked to them often in the North. It seems that they need someone for a job that must be done up north, and they are interested in you. I don't know whether or not they will go any further with this, but at least you have had the chance to be seen."

"But who were they?" Lee asked impatiently.

"They? Why they are the head of intelligence here in Taegu. They are with both the American army and the Korean army. Very important men." Aunt sipped her wine thoughtfully for a moment. "I think that they were impressed. I think that they were very impressed with you. It would seem that they will be back to see you again."

But Lee had a plan forming in his mind. He wanted to try it on his own. Tomorrow he was going to the army company that he had seen today. He would go in and see the head of intelligence, and ask for a job himself.

When he told Aunt the next day what his intention was, she chuckled and warned him not to get arrested. "Your career will end if we have to get you out of jail," she laughed.

With great determination he approached the dust-colored gates of the company the next day. He stopped in front of the Korean guard.

"Excuse me," Lee asked politely, "where will I find the office of army intelligence?"

"Do you have a pass?" The guard looked at him coldly.

"No. I want to ask about work. I want to work for the intelligence office."

"No one can enter without a pass." The guard turned away. Lee saw that it was useless to argue. He crossed the street to think about it. As he watched the gate, a truck turned in and stopped. Lee watched the guard go over to the driver and check his papers. More trucks were coming down the street. Lee waited until they too had turned into the gate. He darted across the street, and while the guard was busy with the drivers' papers he ran through the gate hiding behind the trucks. Going quickly down the company street, he looked back and saw that the guard had not noticed him. Lee thought, "A man who does his work so well will be blessed in heaven." He jumped happily out of the way of a jeep that beeped angrily at his being in the road, and as he walked he looked around him. Many things were happening all at once. In a nearby field men were drilling. He could hear their sergeant's voice shouting orders as they marched forward, reversed, turned to the side, and then went forward again. Clouds of dust hung in the air from the many jeeps and trucks that moved up and down the streets. There was the sound of loud talk, and music from a nearby barracks. Lee looked at the signs over the various low stucco buildings. Many of them were in both Korean and in English, and that made the job much easier.

Then he saw the one for which he was looking. Bright red letters on a white background said, *Intelligence. Unauthorized personnel, KEEP OUT.*

He cheerfully entered the forbidden door. A tall American was sitting at the desk just inside. Across the room, a Korean sergeant was working. Lee went to the Korean and explained why he was there. At the first words, the sergeant looked extremely angry.

"You cannot read? The sign on the door says keep out. Why do you come in here?" He turned very red.

"What is the trouble?" The American sergeant came up behind Lee, and spoke in Korean. Lee looked at him in great surprise.

"You can speak Korean?"

"Yes, I can speak a little." The GI smiled. "What can we do for you?"

"I want to know about intelligence work. Some Koreans work for you, I am told. They go to the North and get information. I want to know about that. Perhaps I can help." The words tumbled out of Lee, and he began to feel very nervous.

"Well, young man." The American sat down at his desk, waving Lee to a seat. "Why don't you start at the beginning and tell me how you thought of all this, and how you got by the guard at the gate."

Lee told how he had thought of all this up north, and how, when his father had been captured, he wanted to do something but had to take care of his family. When he mentioned the two men that had come to Aunt's house, he saw the American looking at him sharply, but the GI said nothing until the whole story was finished.

"I see," he said when he had heard all. "And you want to be in the intelligence organization just like that, Hmmmm?" The man tilted back in his chair, and gazed thoughtfully at Lee. After a while he said, "Well, first we have to find out something about you. Then I shall have to talk with the two men that visited you the other night. So, you see, there is usually a long wait before any man is actually assigned for duty."

"But what about the enemy? They will not wait for you to do all of this."

"That is why war is such a slow business." The GI smiled. "I like what you are doing, though. It is very wise of you to learn English. I suspect that you will be able to use it to great advantage. It is beginning to look as though you will have English-speaking people in your country for a long while. And, who knows, you may one day go to America."

"Oh, no. I would not be able to do that. It is too far away.

How would I get there?" The idea delighted Lee, but it seemed so impossible that he did not give it any thought beyond a few dreams.

"Well you never can tell."

"Then I will talk more with those two men?"

"I would. See what they have to say. Then we will get together and talk more about the actual plan."

"I have to go back to my aunt's house now. It is lunch time and she is expecting me."

"O.K. I'm going into town. Mind if I walk along with you?" He stood up and reached for his hat as Lee nodded eagerly.

Together they walked down the company street, and the amazed look on the guard's face delighted Lee as they strolled past the sentry box.

"He doesn't believe his eyes. Did you see how he looked?" Lee questioned happily.

"Yes. I guess you really surprised him." The sergeant chuckled. "You're just full of surprises, aren't you?" They both laughed.

As they walked along, Lee chattered about the time he and his family came here on the train. He enjoyed talking to the American, and as soon as he could he switched the language to English so that he could practice what he was learning.

"Hey, you speak pretty well," the sergeant said.

"I have been practicing for a long time. I want to learn more, but I have to speak it and hear it before I can learn to use it better."

"Well, maybe I can help you. We have a group of house-boys in my company that get together. They have been getting men in the company who are interested to teach them some of the basic things about the language. They usually meet twice a week. Like the idea?" Lee nodded enthusiastically.

"Yes, I like that idea very much."

"Fine. The next time that they are going to meet, I will send someone to bring you. Where do you live? Near here?"

"It is quite near here." Lee led the man down a few short streets, and then turned into the one that his aunt lived on. "Here." He pointed to the house. Sergeant Dane took a card from his pocket and a ball-point pen and handed them to Lee. "Write down the address." Lee scribbled the address in Korean, then wrote it very carefully in English.

"Oh, I see. Good. Now I have to be going. I'll be seeing you soon." With a wave the sergeant was off, and Lee went into the house. Kicking off his shoes at the door, he called, "Aunt, I'm home."

"And about time, too." His aunt's voice came from the

depths of the house. She didn't really sound angry, but to be sure, he hurried to find her.

She was sitting in the middle of a pile of books in the study. Her hair was hanging in straggling wisps around her moon face, and she peered up at him through her steel-rimmed spectacles as he entered.

"You see?" She waved at the disordered pile of books. "These came for you while you were out. Some friends of mine discovered them in the next town, and they brought them all over this morning." She interrupted herself to ask, "Where on earth have you been?" But without waiting for an answer, she went right on, "Oh, there are so many lovely books, and most of them in English. Here," she commanded, "look."

He did not hesitate to dive into the inviting pile. He laughed as he dug through them, and was delighted to find many titles that he had never seen before. Occasionally Aunt would hand him one saying, "Oh, look at the pictures in this!" or, "What a lovely binding, here, look."

It wasn't until after their very late lunch that he had the chance to tell her about what had been happening to him that morning. She listened with awe to his tale, and told him how brave he must be to walk up to the company like that.

"And there are classes that I may go to to learn to speak

English. The sergeant is going to send for me so that I can go to the next one."

"All this reminds me of tonight. Speaking of messages, those two gentlemen are coming tonight after dinner. They want to talk to you again." She laughed at Lee's excited gasp. "Yes, they should be here about seven."

Lee spent a wonderful day with the books, while Aunt concentrated on getting the house in order for the two men. They ate a hasty supper, and then they sat waiting impatiently for the guests.

At exactly seven, there was a knock at the door, and Lee knew that his big adventure was beginning.

It began slowly, the talk was about many things, and again Lee was aware that the two men were watching him closely. The talk turned to war, and Lee found it hard to contain himself. He spoke quickly, urgently about what the country must do to stop the enemy. They listened to him, and he found himself talking, perhaps too much.

But as the curfew hour drew near, he began to realize that these two men understood what he felt, and why he wanted to do this work.

"I think that you had better stop in and see me tomorrow. I will be at this address." The one called Pahk stood up and handed Lee a card. "I think if you stop in around ten tomor-row morning." He smiled and shook hands with Lee. They both bowed good night to Aunt, and left.

"You hear? I think they are going to let me work with them." He laughed aloud at the thought.

"You know," his aunt said seriously, "you have to go to the farm and tell Choo."

"Yes," the thought sobered Lee, and he sat down. "Yes, I hadn't thought about that. I think that I will wait until I know for sure just what I am going to do." He stood up slowly. "You know, there is nothing decided yet. It may turn out to be a dream. Perhaps our army will make this whole idea unnecessary. There are so many things that might change. Yes, I think it is best to wait and make certain that these things we are thinking of are going to happen. Then I will go to the farm. We won't worry her without cause."

"Is it so hard to talk to her?" Aunt looked at him, one eye-brow cocked.

"Yes." He said simply.

VI Without Promise to Meet Again

THE NEXT morning Lee went to the address on the card. He found the place in an old run-down business building. Climbing a flight of rickety steps to the second floor, he entered the office at the top. Mr. Pahk was sitting behind a huge, battered desk. He stood up when Lee peered around the door.

"Good morning." Mr. Pahk extended his hand in the Western style. "Come sit over here and we will continue our talk."

Again he let Lee talk about the things that interested him,

and his plans for the future. Then he almost abruptly changed the subject. "Now, down to business. I am convinced that, with the proper training, you might do very well for a special job that I have in mind. The only thing that we really have to watch is time. This operation is big, and the time is running out." He stopped and lit a cigarette, leaning back in his chair.

"You see, our sources in the North tell us that there is going to be a major military offensive in late January or early February. That gives us a very short time to prepare you and to get you up to Seoul."

"What kind of training do you mean?" Lee asked.

"Well, first we have to make sure that you are in good physical condition. From what you tell me about your work on the farm, I would guess that you are in peak condition now. The next thing is to teach you a few tricks about the enemy so that you won't make any stupid mistakes. You will be a Communist while you are traveling, and there are things you should know about their operation, and the way that they do things. That means a lot of class work. That means that you have to study certain materials and learn them letter perfect."

"I think that I can do that. I was always good in school at learning things." Lee was glad that he had gotten good marks, now. It made him feel that he could take all this new material, and learn it.

"Yes. We know that you did well. We will show you how to handle the necessary equipment that you will need to know about. We will teach you only those things you will need to know. No more. There isn't time for more. You will be shipped off to Seoul as soon as you have learned the things we wish you to know. Now, is there anything that you have to do that will take time?"

Lee told him that he would have to go to his grandmother's farm to tell his mother. Pahk listened sympathetically. When Lee had finished, he nodded. "I think that it would be wise not to tell her too much. Just say that you are going to school, and that you may go back home. No more." Lee was surprised at the sharp way Pahk said those last two words. He was beginning to find the hard authority that lay beneath the charm of this man. Lee nodded, and that was all for then.

Lee left, promising to report immediately after his return from the farm. He knew that the difficult part still lay before him. Telling Choo would be the hardest thing he had ever had to do in his life. There was no sense putting it off. He would go tomorrow.

When he told Aunt, she agreed that it was best to leave

soon. He left a message with her for the sergeant, should he come in his absence.

The morning was bright and he walked rapidly, remembering that exercise would keep him in good condition. It was only when he drew near the farm, that his steps began to lag. But then, putting his fears behind him, he strode on to the little thatched house sitting on the edge of the rich fields.

It was late that afternoon before he had a chance to tell Choo quietly what he had planned, or at least part of what was planned. At first Choo was very upset, and then she began to see that this was not a boyish whim. It was a man's business, and her son had come very close to being a man. But the woman in her rebelled. "You are too young. Your older brother is in the army, and we haven't heard anything from him in months. Your father is gone. Am I now to lose you in this foolish business? You will make me sorry that I ever had babies before you are all through with me." She turned from him and left the room.

"I must do what I can," Lee said following her. "I am too young for the army. That is true. But here is something that I may be able to do." His words were pleading with her for understanding. "I wish that you would understand that I have to do this."

"I have seen much of man's foolishness in my life." Choo

sounded very tired. She spoke almost in a whisper, looking directly at her son. "I have lived with the Japanese and all the danger that was there. I have gone through the occupation, and now this war. I have borne a child in this war. I have seen my husband torn from me, and my first son is gone. All for this thing called country."

"Are you not proud of them . . . of what they tried to do?"

"Yes, yes. I am proud of their strength, their courage. But that is small comfort to a woman when she begins to lose everything." Tears came to her eyes. "I only seek to keep what is left of my family. Do you call that wrong?"

"You must understand." Lee reached out to touch her hand.

"I understand." Choo turned away. "I understand as much as I can, but I feel only despair. I will try to forgive you." She left him standing there, realizing how poor words were when one wanted to say something important.

The next morning with quiet farewells, he returned to Tacgu, and once he entered the city, directed his footsteps to the offices of Pahk. He would begin his training on the next day.

When he got home, Aunt realized what had happened at the farm, and she did not say a word about his trip. Quickly preparing his supper, she allowed him to go off into the den without any talk. When she looked in much later, he had fallen asleep on the couch with a book in his hand. Quietly covering him over, she let him stay there.

At seven the next morning, Lee reported for training, and there followed two of the most amazing weeks that he had ever known. In rapid succession he was introduced to many customs of the Chinese, was taught to recognize the North Korean dialect, and how to imitate it. He learned advanced judo, and pressure techniques, along with how to use small weapons. He was carefully instructed in the art of escaping, eluding dogs, and how to make himself inconspicuous in a strange city. He acquired a whole new identity, and the papers that went with it. It took many days for him to learn all of the facts of his new background, as the identity he had been given had once belonged to a real person.

His days fell into an exhausting routine. In the morning he would have a quick physical workout, then the class sessions. After lunch he would go through equipment checks, and then he would finish the day with the judo class, often getting home thoroughly shaken up from a bad afternoon.

The two weeks sped by. Before he realized it, he was told that he would be on his way into enemy territory at the end of the next week. During that time, he got his enemy uniform, and became familiar with it. He hated the sight of that little cap, the heavily padded jacket, and the rubber-soled canvas shoes. Across his chest he carried two bandoleers filled with his ration of rice.

His aunt surveyed him with horror. "You are going to look like that? What will all our friends say?" She threw up her hands, and went to warm the saki jug.

He was to be driven north to a point just outside of Seoul, which was now held by the Communists. They had taken it again on January fourth. From that vantage point, they could launch a mighty attack.

Pahk came to the truck to see him off. "Just remember that you must not fail. You have your instructions, and you know where your contact is to be. Talk to no one unless you know he can be trusted, and even then, do not involve anyone unnecessarily. You have your pass words?" Lee nodded. "Good. Go, then, and don't fail."

Aunt came running out. They had said good-by, but she had forgotten to give him his lunch. She looked at him mournfully, and for the first time since he had known her, she seemed close to tears. He reminded her to go and see his mother, and to take care of herself. She nodded wordlessly, and the truck began to move away. He waved from the cab, and then settled himself for the long trip.

The driver was very quiet as they moved over the rough roads, and Lee had time to think back on the past weeks and ahead to the next few. It seemed a very short time before the driver said, "Now. I will let you out at the next turn. You are about twenty miles from Seoul, and very near the enemy territory. Be careful. Do not forget that they will shoot you before they ask questions."

In minutes Lee was alone on the road, and walking toward the distant city.

The January sun soaked through his clothing as he walked. He moved quickly, his eyes watching ahead for Communist patrols. Often he would touch the thick envelope in his coat pocket that contained his papers. These had to be safe as they had his new identification, and all his travel papers for the enemy territory. They were excellent forgeries, and he should have no trouble passing through the lines into the city.

He thought ahead to the job that he had come here to do. It sounded quite simple. He was to find a place where enemy tanks were grouped together in or near Seoul. The Communists were getting ready for a heavy offensive against the United Nations forces, and the attack was to be spearheaded by a large number of heavy tanks. The army in the South had gotten word that the tanks had been moving slowly down from North Korea, traveling at night to escape detection.

There had been no reliable reports on how many there were, but the number was supposed to be large. The last report had said that the tanks were coming into Seoul for a final check-up before going into battle. From all that the intelligence force could learn, the attack was destined to come in early February.

Lee was to find the spot or spots where these tanks were, and then he was to wait until January twenty-ninth. That was the night that the Americans were going to send a flight of bombers over Seoul. Lee was to send a message of the approximate location, and then on that night, he was to mark the spot, that the bombers might find their target. A very simple task, but fraught with danger. He knew that there was an excellent chance that he would never get back alive. The enemy was watching very closely for just such attempts. He felt the excitement of his mission as he saw Seoul only a short distance away.

He had no trouble getting into the city. He told the sentries that he was a South Korean Communist returning to his company in Seoul after a brief leave to go home. His papers backed up his story, and his honest face left no doubt that he was telling the truth.

How strange it felt to be coming into Seoul after these months away. To see his city more than half destroyed left a sick sadness in him. As he walked through familiar streets, he felt the pain and despair that come from seeing many landmarks in total ruins. But he made his heart hard, and vowed that he would not fail in his job. His work would help end the war that much sooner, and the work of rebuilding the city would begin. Of course, he realized, when the UN forces came again to the capital, the destruction would be even worse as another siege began.

He turned his mind away from these things, and began to think of how he would go about doing his job.

First he must make his contact. He would have to find the man here who would give him the flares he needed, and who would handle the messages to the South. This would have to be done soon, but he would not take the flares until near the end. They were too dangerous to have around.

His first stop was back at his own house. The sun was almost gone as he came to his neighborhood. He walked slowly into the area, and looked carefully to see if anyone was watching the house. The streets were silent. He went down an alley, crossed behind several neighbors' houses, and entered the garden at the rear of his home. He stood in a dark corner of the yard listening. He could see that there were no lights, but this might have been the law.

In the deepening twilight, he listened for sound. Low mur-

murs and the sounds of supper activity came from nearby buildings. He went nearer.

"Mr. Ko," he whispered loudly. He waited. The house seemed to be listening. He whispered the name again.

"Who is there?" The answer came from the window by Lee's head.

"It is I, Lee. I have come from the South. May I come in?"

"Wait, and I will unlock the door."

Lee heard a bolt slide back, and the door slid open.

"Quickly," hissed Mr. Ko, and Lee darted through the opening. The door shut, and then a match scratched, flared, and a candle flame leaped bright and steady. Lee felt a deep happiness surge through him at the sight of the old man's face suddenly illuminated by the light.

"Mr. Ko, it is so good to see you again." They shook hands warmly. "I did not know if you would still be here."

"What are you doing in Seoul? This is a very dangerous place now." Mr. Ko looked worried as he went to the windows to make sure that the curtains were drawn tight. He spoke in a whisper, "The police are everywhere. We must be very careful." He looked sharply at Lee. "You are here for some reason. What is it?"

Lee told him the whole story. Mr. Ko scratched his head and said, "You are the only mad man in a very calm family.

Do you mean that you came up here to do a wild thing like that?" He sighed, shaking his head.

Lee smiled. He knew that the old man would call his work madness. It did not bother him. "Can you help me? You know more about the city and what is happening here than any other man. Can you tell me where to look for the tanks?"

"Ah, just as I remember you. We speak for two minutes and you ask the impossible." He looked at Lee for a moment, "Of course, there are a lot of rumors. But one only learns confusion from rumors." He was searching his mind for related material that would help Lee. "There have been one or two steady whispers about tanks and a new offensive. And recently I have heard of tanks being in the area of the West Gate. That may be what you are looking for." He stopped again to sort out mentally the many bits of information that came to him.

"If I go, is there any way that I can travel safely?" Lee had been thinking of this during the whole journey from the South. How could he move through the streets without being picked up and sent to the army. Surely someone would eventually check on his papers. They would help, but probably would not be enough to keep him safe.

"You must remember one thing," said Mr. Ko coming

closer. "You must remember that the Communist army is made up of peasants and farmers. There are very few clever people in the army, and chances are that you will not be in contact with them. They are the leaders. So, prepare yourself to fool the simple mind. Remember that the simple mind is held by fear. Use that fear."

"How can I do that?" The idea puzzled Lee.

"Young people try too often to be too clever. Use a little trick. It will do more for you than any elaborate plan. You have papers?" Lee nodded. "Then use those only when you are in a desperate situation. For the stupid ones, use a simple trick. Those people are afraid of this war, of the army, and of the secret police. The police send out many men who do nothing but go from point to point with little black books. They write down many things. No one knows what these things are that they write, but they pass without trouble." Mr. Ko smiled for a moment.

"Then you think that if I use a trick like that, I will be able to move about Seoul without detection?" Lee laughed loudly.

"Shhhhh. Not so much noise or you will be discovered within the night." But the old man was grinning widely, too. "Do you have a little notebook?"

"The one that I used in school. It would be just right. It is here in my room." Lee lit another candle and went to his bedroom shielding the flame with his hand. He found the small notebook in a wall cabinet. Yes, this would be perfect.

The next day, he spent cleaning his clothes and preparing for the trip to the West Gate. He had five days to find the place, and to get ready for the planes.

Four days to the date of the raid, as he walked to the West Gate, he found that Mr. Ko was right; the black book worked very well. He was stopped several times by the police, but they let him go when he told them that he was on official business. He held his pencil ready, and occasionally wrote down names or facts in mysterious groups on the notebook's pages. When a guard or policeman would stop him, he would ask the man his name, and make a note in his book. Then he would nod at the man and say, "Good work. I like to see a man on his job. I will see that our leader will remember you." Lee would then walk away leaving a happy man behind. He considered it unimportant that he had no idea who the "leader" was.

He soon saw the West Gate area was one of great activity. Many soldiers were buzzing around, and there was an increase in traffic. Lee knew that the hills west of Seoul were honeycombed with caves and he guessed that many of these were being used to house the men, as he saw no barracks or tents about.

Penetrating more deeply into the area, he came over the brow of a low hill, and found the tanks. They were well covered with camouflage so as to be invisible from the air and were in two rows on either side of the broad road leading back to Seoul. There must have been thirty or forty of them, he thought. Looking at the surrounding territory, he realized that it would be hard indeed to guide the planes to this area. The land on either side of the road was flat, overgrown with weeds. Probably there had once been rice paddies here, but since the war, no one wanted to farm such busy land even if the Communists would let them.

As he watched, Lee slowly noted all the bits of cover, the paths and their relation to the tanks, and the number of men that seemed to be involved with the machines. There were not many men in sight, but this was probably to prevent any attention being drawn to the area should a patrol plane fly over. He noticed that there were also several antiaircraft guns carefully concealed near the tanks. They were ready for anything.

Walking back to Seoul, he thought the problem over carefully. How would he manage to light up the whole column?

It was so long that he would not be able to get from one end to the other and mark the spot with flares as the bombers were flying over. He shook his head and entered the city.

It did not take very long to find the shop of the contact. It was here that he would pick up the flares, and send the radio message to the South. He paused at the door to look up and down the street. He seemed to be just looking in the window, but his eyes, caution-sharpened, took in the whole street. He did not even see the little curios that were piled in the window in great disarray.

Certain that he was not observed, he entered the dim doorway quickly. The shop was gloomy, and the smell of cooked food hung heavily in the air. Lee glanced at the contents of the place, and saw only the ordinary dishes, paper and brass objects that were so familiar to a shop of this sort. At a charcoal fire in the rear, a man was sitting with his back to Lee. He did not turn, but continued to sip from a tiny cup in his hand.

"The rooster crowed loudly this morning," Lee said while examining a small brass bowl ornately carved with lotus flowers.

"The red rooster is an angry bird," the man answered raising his head, but still not turning.

"An angry bird in the Land of the Morning Calm," Lee

answered. The man put down his cup, and stood up looking at Lee for the first time.

"You have been long in Seoul?"

"I have recently come from other parts." Lee waited for a sign of recognition from the sharp eyes that did not once leave his face.

"You have come from far away?" the man reached for his long pipe, and began to put tobacco into the small brass tip.

"Yes. When my work is finished, I will return."

"You have come, then, to do a job?"

"My job is to light up the night sky." Lee began to relax.

"Perhaps I can help you, Mr. Lee."

"How do you know my name?" Lee was very surprised.

"We would be doing a poor job if your name had not reached me by now," said the man smiling a little. "Sit down." Lee sat near the charcoal fire feeling the warmth seeping through his padded jacket. It felt good after the cold outside.

"Would you like tea?" The man was very friendly now, and he bent to move the tea water over the fire. Lee liked the calm face that appeared so ruddy in the charcoal glow. "I have a package for you," the man said as he spilled hot water into a little green teapot. "It will help you do your job." He got another tiny cup for Lee, and in a few moments poured it full of the amber fluid. When both had relaxed more, he asked Lee what had been happening since his arrival in Seoul, and Lee told him all that he had found out that morning.

"They will have a hard target to hit. The tanks are in a long line on both sides of the road to the west of the city. I will have to light up both ends of the row, and they will have to bomb all that is between the two flares."

"How do you plan to work that? You cannot be in two places at once."

"I don't know yet." Lee shook his head. "I don't know, but I will think of something."

"I will have radio contact with them today. Is there anything else you want me to say?"

"Tell them . . ." Lee stopped. For a moment he had wanted to send a message to his mother so that she would know that he was safe, but then this was not the way to do it. The army could not use the radio for personal messages. "No. There is nothing else. I will take the package and go back to my house." He stood up, and waited as the man went to the back of the store and came back a moment later with a heavy package. With a smile of thanks, he went out of the shop.

It was very cold, now, and the milky, late afternoon sun

seemed to have no warmth in it at all. A chill wind blew needle sharp particles of dust against his face as he hurried through the back alleys to his house. Mr. Ko was out when he got there. He hurriedly unwrapped the parcel. It held two flare guns, and six flares. Good, he thought, this will be enough to do the job. Re-wrapping the package tightly, he put it in the bomb shelter under his bedroom floor. It would be safe there even if the house was searched.

Later that afternoon Mr. Ko returned, and Lee told him about the flares, getting one and showing him how they worked.

The old man's eyes showed his interest even though he said, "And with these you are going to defeat the whole Communist army?" He reached down and picked up one of the flare guns. "Very interesting. Hmmmm. And all you have to do is to pull this and the thing will shoot?" He pointed at the trigger.

"Yes," Lee answered fingering the other gun. "Shooting these is very simple. I think that I shall have to make a fuse for one, and shoot the other myself. You see, I have to light up both ends of the tank column at once just as soon as I hear the sound of the planes coming." Lee looked off into space. "It will be a big chance to take."

"What is that?"

"Well, sometimes a fuse does not work. If it fails, then I will fail."

"But it is really very easy." Mr. Ko spoke as though to himself. "I think that it is so easy that even an old man could do it."

"And I think that I can detect your thoughts." Lee looked sternly at the old man. "No. I will not let you do it. That is my last word."

"And if you fail? You must not let your stubbornness stand in the way of success. You cannot afford to fail." Lee realized that the old man spoke the truth. If he failed, it would mean many lives lost, and probably the war would run for many more months. Lee looked at the man saying, "I have much to learn yet. I have yet to learn how to argue with one such as you." He smiled as he spoke, feeling a deep relief that there would be someone with him on this job. It was good to know that the job would be done right.

"You are very wise for one of your years," Mr. Ko said. "You are wise enough to know that no one can be a hero without help."

"Yes," Lee said thoughtfully. Then he turned back to business. "Here let me show you exactly how this will all work." He began to scratch out the plan on paper, and the old man watched carefully, not letting a single detail slip by.

The night of the raid was perfect. A low moaning wind whined in from the west, and the moon was lost behind thick, scudding black clouds. It seemed as though the night had been made for violence, for danger.

Lee shivered against the cold as he crossed the fields outside of Seoul. Stopping for a moment he held his watch close to his eyes where he could just see the luminous dial. There was still time.

Ahead, through the inky night, he could see the blinking lights of the workmen near the tanks. He cut off to the right into the barren rice paddy he had seen four days before. The wind hid the sound of crackling weeds as he moved closer to his destination. For just a moment the moon broke through the racing clouds, and Lee crashed to the earth lying rigid and still. Then the blackness returned, and he leaped up, moving quickly forward.

The clank of metal on metal, and the sound of men talking excitedly was borne to him on the night wind. The tanks were just ahead. Lee edged his way to the side of the road, crawling, now, on his stomach. The excitement in him had died, and a cold calm filled his body as he watched the moving flashlights, and listened to the near voices. Slowly he moved toward the last tank in the line. He fervently hoped that Mr. Ko was now near the first.

A sudden, roaring sound shot a thrill of fear through him. The tank motors were being started. He grew calm again when he realized what the sound was. Reaching inside his jacket pocket, he pulled out the flare gun. He had loaded it at the house, and it now was ready.

Five minutes to go.

He moved closer. The men on this last tank were working on the other side. As he peered through the screen of weeds, a truck jounced to a halt just a few inches from where he lay hidden.

Two minutes to go.

A man jumped out of the truck. Lee raised his head. The truck was empty. He moved around to the back of it. The sound of the tank motors drowned out any sound that he made. A daring idea popped into his head. Peering into the rear of the truck, he could see that a curtain separated the back from the driver's seat.

Thirty seconds.

Lee raised the flare gun. He thought he could hear the rumble of planes through the roar of the tanks. It was hard to tell. Crunching footsteps were approaching.

Lee fired. The sound of the flare gun was lost in the general noise as the truck driver jumped in and ground the starter. The motor spun into life. Lee took a quick look up before diving into the rear of the truck. The flare left a slim finger of red light against the sky. Quickly he slipped another flare into place, and fired again, just as the truck jerked away, and sped up the road. He threw the gun into the weeds at the side of the road, then crouched down behind the driver's seat, making himself as small as possible.

The flares burst against the dark sky with a startling brilliance. A cry went up from the men. Hoarse orders were barked as motors were cut off, and lights extinguished. The truck driver had not noticed anything wrong yet. With the stopping of the tank motors, Lee could hear the distinct growl of bombers above. Raising his head slightly, Lee saw two more flares burst into light farther down the road. The men who had been working on the tanks began running into the near fields. His truck slowed to climb a hill. Feeling that the distance was enough, Lee moved quickly to the tail gate, and jumped to the road, lost his balance and rolled over and over into a ditch at the side of the road. He jumped up, and raced for the cover of some rocks nearby just as a deafening blast tore the night in two. Lee covered his ears, and huddled close to the rocks. Again and again bombs ripped into the tank line. Between the bombings, Lee could hear the hollow double boom of the antiaircraft guns. The planes had passed over. They would return again to strafe their target. He peered around the jagged boulders that sheltered him. He was about five hundred yards away from the burning tanks. This would be the safest place for a while. Then he heard the planes returning. He ducked as the planes swooped down strafing the area with bullets. Again the ground guns were booming. Somewhere above, there was a deep motor cough, a splutter, and Lee saw the sky light up as a plane, on fire and out of control, spun toward the earth to crash, spreading a flaming arc of debris through the night.

A thin cheer went up from one of the gun positions. Lee edged his way slowly back and around the rocks. The sounds of the planes were dwindling into the south. He leaped from the top of the jagged mound, and sprawled into the field below. Picking himself up, he raced across the frozen rice paddy, back toward Seoul.

It was several hours before Lee could get back to his house. Truck loads of police were racing up and down the streets, and patrols were on every corner. Dodging and darting from shadow to shadow, he finally reached his back yard and exploded through the door into the house. He could see a dim light in the far room.

"Mr. Ko, Mr. Ko," Lee ran down the corridor. The old man was comfortably sitting reading a book by the candlelight. He looked up as Lee burst into the room.

"Ah, I was just beginning to worry about you. I am glad to see that you escaped with no damage." He nodded and smiled. Lee could see that his eyes were twinkling.

"But how did you get back here so soon?" Lee asked, amazed at his calm.

"What I do not have in youth, I have in brains. I arrived here safely quite a while ago." The old man smiled to himself. Under Lee's questions, he would not let the secret of his quick return out. He only said, "It was done, and it was well done. Let it go at that." He beamed at Lee, "When the gods have been good to you, you should not reveal their ways." Then he laughed aloud saying, "I never saw such a raid. The poor enemy will be lucky if they can pick their way back north, never mind begin an offensive to the south." Growing serious again, he said, "You must hide. Every house will be searched. They will try to find the persons responsible for this. Probably they will take many hostages. Right now, no matter what papers you have, I would not try to leave Seoul, or even walk on the streets. They will not let a man out of the city. They need every soldier they can find."

"You are right, but do I dare stay here?"

"I am the only one that knows you are here. We have taken good care of that. There can be no leaks. If you stay in the bomb shelter, I will bring you food. They will leave an old man like me in peace as long as I do nothing to attract their attention. I do not have to worry."

"Then would you go to the shop where I got the flare guns, and tell the man there to radio the South that the mission was a success?" Lee took a scrap of paper and quickly wrote down the code conversation, passing it to Mr. Ko. "Here, this is how he will know you. It would be best if you memorized this and burned the paper."

Mr. Ko read the paper, and nodded. "Is there anything else that I should tell them?"

"Yes. Tell them that I am safe. Perhaps they will go to the farm, and tell Mother that everything is all right."

"I will do this tomorrow. Now you had better make that

space under the floor as comfortable as possible. You will probably be there a long time."

"Yes. It will be months before the UN army comes again. We have made a dent in the enemy, but it will be a long time before they can be driven out completely." Lee went to get his bedding and a candle. Lifting the concealed trap door, he jumped down into the damp hole. Without thinking about the days that would come, he wrapped himself in the blankets, and laid down to sleep. He could hear Mr. Ko moving about above his head, and he realized that the man was covering any signs of Lee's presence in the house.

It seemed only a little later that Lee was jolted out of sleep by the sound of a fist crashing on the front door. He heard muffled voices above him, and the thick thumping of heavy boots on the floor. They passed over his head, and he saw the floor shake. He could hear the sounds of a thorough search, as doors were pulled open, and furniture was overturned. Occasionally he could hear Mr. Ko's thin voice whining, "I am an old man. Oh, have mercy, mighty conqueror. Leave a poor old man in peace."

Lee could not help smiling at the sly old man, and he felt triumphant relief when the footsteps and surly voices moved on to the next house. An exhausted sleep claimed him, then, and he dreamed of a great parade through the streets of Seoul. He was riding in an open car, and the people were cheering wildly. He smiled in his sleep.

VII   To Rebuild a Life

THE EXCITEMENT of the raid was over. Lee could not leave the house, and most of the day he had to stay in the bomb shelter. If anyone saw him, they might talk. That would be dangerous. Once the police even heard a whisper of his being in Seoul, they would tear the house apart to find him. It would not take much intelligence to put the bombing raid and his return from the South together and get the obvious answer. So, day after day he ticked the monotonous minutes away. Always he asked Mr. Ko for the latest war news, and always there was nothing new to report. The Communists had cut all communication from the people. The city was in a state of siege-like isolation. Only military personnel were permitted to pass in or out. Even the free radio stations were jammed with noise from Communist transmitters at all times so that no word came from the South.

The days passed into weeks, and the weeks into months. Lee suffered with his confinement, but Mr. Ko began to find books here and there for him to read. That helped a little, but his muscles felt cramped and aching from so long a period of inactivity.

Then, once again, the rumors began to circulate, the rumors that told of a coming attack from the South. Mr. Ko shuffled from place to place bent on his obscure business, and picked up a grain of news here, a grain there. He brought the news back home, and he and Lee would sift it out together finding the fact becoming obvious that the UN was ready for a new attack.

Two weeks later, the guns began in the south, and artillery rained once again on Seoul. This time, the attack was short, and it was only a matter of days until the enemy had been driven out once more. The UN troops swooped through the streets in triumph. There was a great deal of celebrating, but still the question hung in the city, "Would the enemy come

back again?" No person could tell. All saw the parade of
equipment that continued to pour through the city, and kept
going north. All heard the guns slowly moving farther and
farther north. But still the question stayed with the people.

Lee delighted in the new freedom, and daily he went out
into the streets to watch the companies of soldiers move into
the empty compound areas around Seoul. Slowly the streets
filled with refugees coming from the North, and people returning from the South to their homes. The stalls began to
open, and the keepers would shout their wares. The basket
and pottery merchants lined the streets in front of their shops
with goods gaily decorated, and even an occasional bullock
was seen plodding its way among the army trucks and jeeps
as it was walked back toward some nearby farm.

Because the railways had not suffered much damage, the
trains began to travel between Seoul and Pusan with fair reg-
ularity. Lee realized that soon Choo would be coming home
to find out what had happened. He had gone to the shop of
the man with the radio as soon as the enemy had been
driven out, but he had found the man gone. In his place was
an old papa-san who knew nothing of radios or intelligence
operators, all he knew was that he had rented the shop for
several months to a very nice young man who paid his rent
promptly.

With the radio gone, there was no way to reach Taegu. He had only to wait until Choo heard that the city was free and safe again, and returned home.

Lee realized that now peace had come to the city he would have to get a job to help support the family when they did arrive. He checked with all of his father's friends, but they were not started in business enough to hire, or they remembered his raid on their finances when he needed money to go south, and so were unwilling to hire such an unorthodox person. As Lee listened to their many excuses, he realized that he would have to pay back the money as soon as he could to satisfy them, and to restore his reputation. This would not be as difficult as before. Inflation was setting in. This meant that money would be worth less, and that there would be a great deal more of it.

But that still did not give him a job, and finding one was the next major project for him to tackle. One day while watching the stream of jeeps and trucks flowing by, he suddenly thought that the best thing to do would be to work for the army. If he could get a job in a company, that would solve his problems right there. They paid better than any other job he might find, and he would have a chance to practice speaking English. But, because jobs with the army were in great demand, he would have to hurry to find one that he could have. Then he remembered Pahk from the South. Surely he would be somewhere in Seoul either now or soon. He would be able to help him. Lee went quickly to where Mr. Ko was setting up his new shop. He found the man nailing shelving into place.

"Mr. Ko, I think I have an idea for getting a job," Lee burst into the tiny shop. "I will go to the intelligence office, and talk to Mr. Pahk if he has come back to the city." Lee handed Mr. Ko the next board to be nailed.

"That sounds like a fine idea. All that remains is to find the intelligence office. It could be anywhere in Seoul. I think that you might try the police station. Speak to a friend of mine there. Here, I will write his name down for you. He knows everything that is happening in the city, and I know he has come back." Mr. Ko scrawled a name on paper and handed it to Lee.

That was the beginning. Through the police, Lee found Mr. Pahk, and Pahk arranged to have Lee start working in an American company near his home within the week. The work was hard, but simple. His duties were to keep the barracks clean, take the soldiers' clothes to the laundry, and generally run any errands that needed to be done. He also had to bring in the water cans full every morning, as there was no other supply beyond the fat Lister bag that hung in the yard.

He had never seen one before, and it fascinated him that a bag could be filled with water and a chemical that took all impurities out of the water making even the most dangerous liquid safe.

Choo and the children came from the South. By this time Lee had his job down to a simple routine, and she marveled that he had gotten such a well-paying position.

Lee often had time on his job to read the pocket books that were laying around the barracks. When he could not get the meaning of a word from the sentence, he could ask one of the soldiers to help him. One day, laboring over a history book, he came to the phrase "in some cases . . ." He knew that cases were boxes for packing things in, but that didn't seem to fit this sentence. He looked around the barracks to see who was there that might help him out. A soldier was lying half dressed on his bed reading an ancient copy of *Life*.

"Frank," Lee handed the book to the GI, "what does it mean *in some cases?*"

"Let's see." Frank glanced over the paragraph, "Mmmmm. Well, that's hard to explain." He scratched his head and gave the book back. "Look, I'm a little busy now, but you come back later and we'll see if we can figure it out."

He yawned and began looking at the picture magazine again. Lee stood up a little disappointed. He turned away.

"What is it?"

Lee turned to the voice. It was the new GI. He had come into the radio company yesterday. He sat on his bunk writing a letter, and without looking up had extended a hand for the troublesome book. "Let me take a look." He continued to write, finishing the sentence.

"Now." He read the page, glanced over the book, and then asked, "Where is your English-Korean dictionary?" His sharp eyes scanned Lee's face, one eyebrow raised quizzically.

"I no have." Lee produced the only dictionary that he did have, a worn, paper-bound Korean-English book.

"Can you afford to buy another?" The GI lit a cigarette. Lee shook his head. "I see." The soldier buttoned up his fatigue jacket and reached for his cap. "Come on. You show me where the bookstores are. We will see what we can do." He got up and started out the door. Lee jumped to his feet and followed quickly.

As they walked down the company street to the gate, the GI said, "My name is Bill. I know yours, Lee. This little walk is no trouble for me. I wanted to go to the PX anyway. I imagine that the book stalls are nearby."

"Yes. They are near." Lee said nothing for a few minutes, and they passed out through the gate, down the crooked dirty street to the main avenue. "The first one is only a short way down this street." He pointed ahead to a row of low shops that lay ahead.

"Fine. I don't imagine that there are many books in these shops. It's too soon after the attacks." He began to whistle. Lee noticed that Bill's eyes were moving over every building that they passed, they took in the face of every person on the street. This was unusual to him as he was used only to those soldiers who saw very little, but said a great deal. He glanced out of the corner of his eye at Bill who strode along beside him. Bill was very tall, and his light hair shone in the hot sunlight when he took off his fatigue cap to wipe his forehead. Lee noticed that the eyebrow was still cocked in the same attitude as at the barracks, but under the slightly skeptical look it gave him, there was a sadness lurking deep in the hazel eyes. That caught Lee's curiosity at once, and his sympathy. He liked the straight nose and the high pronounced cheekbones in the thin face. They had a clean, clear-cut look, and strengthened the full, wide mouth.

"What's your decision, doctor?" Bill glanced down at the little figure beside him. Lee blushed, having the feeling that his thoughts were being read. He smiled and said, "Good."

Bill nodded, and pointed to the shop near them. "That looks like a likely place. Let's try it." He swung through the narrow door, and walked to the back of the store where two men were playing a very complicated game with white and black pieces of ivory. He stood there a moment, but neither man seemed to notice him.

"I guess this is a self-service shop," he said, smiling at their concentration, and he went to the rows of books on the shelf nearest him. He quickly spotted an Atlas, and handed it to Lee. Without comment, he went to the shelf holding dictionaries. Leafing through several, he selected one saying, "This should meet our needs."

An elderly lady came from the back of the store and approached them. Bill nodded and smiled at her. She beamed back, and came forward to help if she could. She murmured something softly in Korean.

"What did she say?" Bill asked Lee.

"She welcomes you to her shop, and hopes that she may serve you."

"Tell her thank you for me, and tell her we will take those two books." Lee translated the words into Korean, and the lady beamed more broadly. She came closer and patted Bill's arm, a kindly smile on her face. Then she turned to Lee and they began to talk while Bill continued to look through the shelves, occasionally picking up another paper-bound book.

"Here. I think that these will hold you for a while." He handed three more that he had found to Lee. One was a geography of the world, one an American history book printed in Korean, and one was a book on English grammar. Bill pointed to the grammar book saying, "It's a foul, but necessary item. You will learn most by practice, but this will help you keep the words straight. There is a list of spelling words in the back for what it is worth." He reached into his pocket, and took out a roll of Korean money. "Ask the lady how much we owe her." When he had paid, he commented, "I don't often go out and spend fifteen hundred in the afternoon. It is a good thing that your Korean won and our dollar have a lot of space between." In American money, that is about a dollar and a half." He stuffed the rest of the money into his pocket, and they waved good-by to the lady, leaving the shop.

Lee began leafing through the books as soon as they were on the street. He excitedly pointed out the pictures of events he had read about, the signing of the Declaration of Independence, the Gettysburg Address, and many others.

"These books will help whoever is teaching you to get all the main points that you should know. If you can digest these books, learn what is in them, then you will be well on your way to understanding more and more."

"But, I teach myself. Look. I can find cases in my dictionary, now. See? It is here. The def . . . def . . ."

"Definition."

"Yes, definition is here in Korean language so that I can understand." He glanced through the dictionary happily, and when they came to the PX he sat down outside reading while Bill went inside to do his shopping.

The PX stood at the head of a huge square that was filled with people. Many GIs walked leisurely by the endless open stalls where the owners all shouted their wares. In some there were cameras, in others simple or ornate brass work, in most there was just a motley collection of junk from hinges to toilet bowls sitting in undignified exposure to the public eye. The shouts of the vendors made each article seem to be a jewel beyond price. But Lee's ears had grown so used to this noise, it did not disturb him. Occasionally he glanced up and took in the square with a quick look, but he went right back to his book after resting his eyes for a second. About half an hour later Bill came down the steps of the squat, graystone building. He carried two brown paper sacks. Lee saw him and jumped up.

"Ready?" Bill asked as he drew near. Lee nodded, and they began walking away. "Wait," Bill said, looking at the shops across the street. "I think that we should take a look over there while we are in town." He crossed the street and began to tour slowly through the various stalls, stopping to examine more closely the things that caught his eye. At one booth, he saw a pair of sunglasses. Trying them on, he turned to Lee. "How do they look?"

"Fine." Lee dreaded what was going to happen next. This man was a stranger in Korea. He would not know how to bargain. He would pay too much for them.

"How much," Bill asked the man selling the glasses.

"Fourteen dollar." The reply came promptly.

"No. Nope. Can't do it." Bill shook his head slowly, looking at the glasses with regret on his face.

"They are very fine. Very fine."

"Yes. They are nice."

Lee listened with growing unhappiness. Didn't he know that you had to pretend not to want the stuff? Here he was

telling the salesman that it was a fine object. Bill looked at
Lee for a moment. He was still shaking his head. Lee knew
he must not interrupt.

"You speak, how much," the salesman indicated his will-
ingness to dicker.

"Well I had thought about four dollars." His words threw
the vendor into an hysteria of words. He waved his arms, and
called upon all of the gods of the market place to defend him
against such a thief. Bill listened politely, and then began to
look towards a neighboring booth. The vendor sensed im-
pending disaster. He spoke quickly interrupting his own ti-
rade. "Nine dollar. I give to you for nine dollar." He nodded
to himself, looked around to see who else was noticing his
burst of generosity.

"Six dollars." There was a tone of finality in Bill's voice.
Lee looked up at him. There was growing admiration on his
face as he watched a master at the art of haggling fan six one
dollar bills in GI scrip money out in his hands. He picked up
the glasses, and held both hands out to the stall keeper. The
man looked from the hand with the glasses to the hand with
the money, and then in desperation took the six dollars with
an exclamation of disgust at his own weakness.

"Does a case come with these?" the question came coolly,

and Lee was overwhelmed. The vendor gazed in open-mouthed amazement at Bill, and without a word, handed him a thick felt case for the glasses.

"Thank you. Good-by." Bill nodded politely, and turned away. Lee followed at his heels, watching him shine the glasses on his handkerchief, then slip them on looking all around to test them out.

"You have never been to Seoul before yesterday?" Lee asked the question in frank disbelief. Where else could a GI learn to bargain so masterfully. Lee would have gotten the glasses for eight dollars, possibly even for seven after long hard work. But to get them for *six!* He followed the broad straight shoulders through the thickening crowd around the PX. This was indeed an unusual man.

When they reached the barracks, Bill asked Lee if he ever got in to see the company movie that was held two or three times a week in the mess hall. Lee told him that he had always wanted to see the American movies, but a GI had to take him into the company after dark. The sentry would allow no one to pass without a GI to vouch for him.

"They start at 7:30. Want to see one tonight?"

"Yes." Lee nodded excitedly. "Yes. I will be at the back gate. You will meet me there?" He grinned at Bill's nod, and they said good-by.

Lee hurried home and waited impatiently for his supper. Choo noticed the new excitement, and enjoyed hearing about the night movie. She had been addicted to the American movies that came to Seoul before the war. She wished that she, too, might go, but did not press the point.

Lee ate quickly, and was ready to get started at seven o'clock. He walked up the alley to the barbershop that had re-opened there. Some of the small children from the nearby houses were playing in the dusty street. Their cries as they ran to and fro echoed down the darkening street. From the close houses grouped like gossiping women huddled together, came the smells and sounds of the early evening. Lee liked the feeling of his street at night. With the darkness a new mystery came over the area, and all looked changed as though by some sorcerer. The dim candlelight shining from the many open stalls cast flickering oases of light in little yellow puddles along the way, and voices would call out to him from the softly lighted booths as he was recognized by the old mama-sans and children that kept watch for late customers. The air was thick with a heavy, sweet smell of frying foods, perfume, and moist earth.

As he walked, slowing his steps to inhale the smells of his neighborhood, he remembered that the air at the farm had never been like this. Probably his grandmother was thinking of just this odor when she referred to the dirty city. But Lee liked the rich scent that was almost touchable around him. He listened for a moment to the sounds of a phonograph grinding out "China Night" in one of the houses nearby. He heard the heavy loud laughter of soldiers. The trees whispered in the slight breeze. He looked up at the roof of leaves that curved dark and mysterious overhead. He couldn't see through to the sky. It was like walking through a dark cave.

He emerged from his street near the company, and made directly for the rear gate. Bill was standing there leaning against the guardhouse, talking quietly with the sentry. He saw Lee, and waved. They went down the company street together to the mess hall.

Lee was surprised that so few soldiers were in the makeshift theater. He asked Bill where they all were.

"Oh, many of them go up the hill to the company club, and some of them slip out of the company on various — ah, errands." As he finished, the lights were cut off, and with a great deal of flickering, the movie began.

Lee had a little trouble following the story, which concerned itself with gangsters, a large city, and a beautiful girl who was always getting into trouble. There was a great deal of shouting and shooting. He marveled at the huge city and the luxurious surroundings. When it was over, he beamed happily at Bill and said that he had enjoyed it.

"Did you understand it, though?"

"Not all. But it was good."

That seemed to satisfy Bill, and he walked back to the gate with Lee. As they came up the hill toward the barracks, Bill said, "Who did you say was teaching you to learn from your books?"

"I am learning myself. I started when down in Taegu, and now I keep on."

"Maybe I could help. I'm on duty tomorrow when you finish, but after that I will be able to work with you. Why don't I come up to your house."

"Yes." Lee agreed, but he was feeling a little uncomfortable. He had seen in the movies how the Americans lived. What would Bill think of his poor house? He did not speak, though, and just said thanks for the movie, and that he would see Bill tomorrow at about seven. He pointed up the street to show where he lived.

"You turn at the barbershop. I will be there waiting." With a quick good night, he hurried off up the street.

The next evening at seven, Lee saw the GI striding up the street and he ran through the twilight to meet him.

"Hi, there," Bill called. Together they walked down the alley to Lee's house. Bill stopped and began to unlace his boots. Lee tried to tell him that it really wasn't necessary for him to do that.

"Don't be polite, young man. Everyone here takes off their shoes before entering a house. I shall, too."

Lee began to see that he could not treat this man like a guest. Bill would have none of it. With this knowledge, Lee's discomfiture disappeared, and he felt better. They went down the hall to the big central room. Earlier, Lee had arranged all the books in the bookcase, and he had cleared the big mahogany desk for work.

"This was my father's room. He worked in here very often."

"What happened to him?"

Lee told Bill how his father had disappeared, and some of the other things that had happened in the war. He did not mention the spy work, nor his shooting a man. Those things were for the past.

It was a few minutes before nine when Bill looked at his watch and said it was time to stop. They had just gotten into the American Revolution, and Lee hated to stop, but the curfew was at nine sharp. No one could be on the streets after that hour.

Slowly Lee began to learn and practice his new knowledge, but it was still quite difficult to speak and make sense. Often Bill would ask him if he wanted to go with him as "interpreter" on errands to the supply depots across Seoul or in Yungdongpo, the city across the Han River. Lee would point out excitedly the places where important events had happened during the war, and the words would get hopelessly scrambled. He would have to try again. Bill would chuckle, and help occasionally, but usually just let him try to think through the sense of the sentence that bothered him. Lee appreciated that. It was hard to do, but it gave him the practice he wanted and needed.

Walking or driving around Seoul, working in the house after dinner, and sometimes stopping for a movie, these were the things that Lee did now. He tried to form goals to work for, but that was hard. He wanted to go back to school, but his family needed the money and food that he earned at the company. There was no night school. He would just have to postpone his plans for another few months, and see what happened. He told Bill this, and the man was sympathetic. He could understand why Lee wanted to go back to school. There wasn't much of a future for one who didn't have a definite knowledge of some trade or profession. Lee began to tell him of all the plans that had been made down south at

Aunt's house, and how he wanted to find some way to carry them out. Bill listened as Lee told more and more of himself and what he had done during the war. Lee mentioned the intelligence men that he knew.

"What about them? They might be able to help you get to school on a scholarship or something."

"They have left the city and gone north. They were needed up there along the line. I am waiting for them to come back. They should be here after the coming winter. But, that is a long time away," Lee said wistfully.

"Well, you remember how you had to wait for things to happen, and you knew they weren't going to happen for a long time?"

"You mean like the favorite holidays?"

"Sure. You just lean back and make yourself busy with other things. Then the time goes by fast, and you don't even notice it. Suddenly you wake up, and there is the special day. Just like that."

"I know," Lee grinned. "That is just the way it happen."

It was very strange. Lee could understand this soldier. He could understand how he felt, and many times, how he was thinking. This was not true of the other GIs. Some of them were very difficult to understand. He could not see why they did not take more of an interest in Korea. Surely they had not traveled very much in their lives. They always talked about their homes, as though they had never been anywhere else. Yet they rarely left the company, preferring to stay with the comfortable and the familiar.

"If I were in your country," Lee thought, "I would want to see everything. I would want to go everywhere."

He was telling Choo about the difference in GIs one night, and she laughed at him. "Surely you know that most people are like that. They don't want something strange and new. They like the comfortable old way much better. They like to see what they know, do what they have always done. I am that way. Even visiting my mother's farm, I longed to set up my own home, and to have my own life back again."

"But sometimes that is not possible. For these Americans, the army has changed that, and they have to leave their homes. They should take advantage of the time to learn about us and the way we live here. There are too few like Bill. He is very different."

"There are too few like you, son, who see these things so clearly. I can say that I am proud of my son. You have come through adversity well. You have not done anything that I would call wrong." She smiled at him. "And I know how badly you want to go to school. I know that there are many ways to make much money in Seoul."

Lee looked at her. There was a light of admiration in his eyes. He had always thought of her as sheltered from the harsh realities of life as it had become in the city. "How did you know what is going on there?" he asked wonderingly.

"Oh, I hear talk. The black market is operating in the open now, and there are many other ways to pick up fast money." She shook her head. "Remember the story I told you?"

Lee nodded, "About the white tiger?"

"Yes. Well, we know it was just a story, but the moral is true. It would not surprise me if you were as pure as that man who rode the white tiger."

"I have tried, Mother." Lee said quietly.

VIII Walk to a Mountain Valley

LEE HAD almost succeeded in pushing the war completely into the background. Occasionally he had dreams that left him frightened and sodden with sweat, when he would start from sleep in terror at some phantom pursuing him across the shadowy plains of night. But these were ghosts of a past that seemed to be well gone. His days were full of work and learning, and where his father and then Mr. Ko had been his teachers, now Bill had taken over with a kindness and warmth that was entirely new to him.

There was a quick sympathy, an enveloping gentleness that clung to this big GI. He would always speak quietly to Lee, and never seem to be irritated by the little mistakes that came while Lee tried to learn the new language. Somehow Bill seemed to sense just what it was that Lee had been through in the war, and he tried to show that, beside the harsh side of life, there was a rich and wonderful side that was too often forgotten. He seemed to realize, too, that Lee, like all young- sters at that age, needed an ideal, a hero to look up to. And in his way, he supplied that need.

But such things are very fragile in a land torn by war. And, as if to remind them that the life could change at any mo- ment, there was the monstrous sound of guns in the north as the war raged only a few dozen miles from the capital. The sound was always present. It beat a soft tattoo of alarm be- hind every daily action, behind every daily talk.

And then the fear was no longer shadowy as in his dreams. The fear became a decision and then it became an action.

The summer had passed into dwindling autumn, and with the falling leaves an early cold wave gripped the land. Bill and Lee were working in the barracks over some new books that they had found in the stalls in Seoul. Bill had been un- usually quiet, and often would look out the window at the harsh frozen compound as it lay in the watery late fall sunlight.

"There is something that you find difficult to say?" Lee asked, slowly putting the history book to one side.

Bill lit a cigarette, and said, "Yes, there is something." He blew a thin stream of smoke into the air, and then said, "Are you all finished with your work here?" Lee nodded. "Then let's go for a walk. We will climb to the top of the hill behind the company, and there we will talk." He stood up and reached for his heavy jacket, and cap. Lee hurried to get his things, and together they went up the company street, by the sentry at the gate, and walking quickly to keep warm, they followed the cobblestoned street to the small square near the compound. As they had done many times before, they climbed the steps from the square to the bare hillside above.

Higher and higher they went, in silence passing by the tiny mud houses that dotted the hillside, by the patches of frozen brown weeds that had been gardens earlier. They came to the upper road that wound around the hill. Still they did not speak, and Lee felt a spark within him ignite and become a burning fear. Bill walked as usual, looking from side to side, taking in all that he saw.

The houses became more ornate as they moved from the

bare hillside to the sheltered side where grew the tall pine trees that they both loved. They left the road and scrambled up the steep hill to the spot they had found that summer. Below this sheltered cove, they could see the whole city of Seoul spread out before them. Today it was cold and blue with thin smoke. Here and there the dim sunlight would glance off icy grass and explode into diamond colors. They sat down on a rough wooden bench. Then Bill began to tell him what had happened.

"One of our communications teams has been wiped out up by Bunker Hill. We are sending a new one out to replace it. I am going as the team chief in charge of operations. We leave in a couple of days."

The pain inside of Lee was a living animal, gnawing at him.

"So, I guess that the lessons have to come to an end for a while, but we can pick them up again when I come back." He flicked the ash of his cigarette, and looked thoughtfully out over the city. "How long have I been here? A couple of months, so far." Lee nodded wordlessly.

"We have done quite a lot in those few weeks. I think that you have been coming along just fine. I know that you can keep on with your lessons even though I am not here to help for a while." He ground the cigarette out under his heel.

"I can go?" Lee's voice shook. He knew what the answer would be.

"No. They won't let us take a houseboy. I . . . I have already tried to get you travel papers. I knew that you would want to come." For the first time he looked at Lee. "They wouldn't give me any. They said that we could get someone up there. You have to have the papers, or you would be picked up by the police, and they would send you back." Lee could see the unhappiness on Bill's face.

"How far is it?" Already Lee's mind was beginning to work again. There must be some way. There had to be.

"It's almost sixty miles. Quite a ways."

"I will walk. If they don't let me go with you, I walk." Lee had decided.

"You would be arrested long before you got there. They are looking at everyone's papers, checking for guerrillas. If you didn't have papers, they might put you in jail." Bill stood up. "You don't want that, do you?" But his words fell on deaf ears. If this was the only way, then this was the way that Lee would go.

"But I must go. If you show me on the map, I will be able to find you."

"You know, I will be back in Seoul after a while," Bill said gently. "I can see you then. Why don't you wait?" Lee shook his head. He wouldn't listen.

"It is very hard to say. You have teach me much, and you have helped me and my family." He pointed down to the heavy army clothes that hung on his small body. "You have given me these clothes so that I would not be cold. You are my friend, and now I must help you." Lee searched for the right words. "Korea is a strange country for you. You have not seen war yet. When you go north, the guns will be loud. Maybe the Communists will come. You will be afraid . . ."

"No," Bill laughed. "Me afraid?"

"Yes, I think. When Communists bomb Seoul, I was very afraid. I hide in my house, and all the time I want to cry. I never tell anyone this, but it is true. All the time I think, maybe I will die. Yes, even when I helped the soldiers I was afraid."

"But that was different. You were all by yourself. You didn't have an army to fight with you."

"Not different," Lee said quietly. "When a man looks at death, he is alone. It is always the same. There is no different." Lee allowed none of his feelings to show, but deep inside a panic churned, a fear that he would not be able to go no matter how he argued.

"I am afraid for you. I go because I know I can help."
Memories flooded upon him, and he remembered too many
good-bys. A brief picture of his father flashed into his head.

"But what if you do come, and while you are there, suppose there is an attack. What will you do then?"

"I have thought of that," Lee answered looking steadily at
Bill.

"We may die," Bill said flatly.

"And if I am not there, and you die? Would that be easier
for me? What would I do then? You die, then I die. No difference." Lee's words were urgent now as he said, "Teacher
once in school said that man is like a country. Alone, he is no
good. Alone he is like a tree, long time no rain comes. If
there is no rain, then the tree dies. It dies slowly, but it dies. I
am like a tree. With your kindness and knowledge, you are
like the rain. You have given me new life . . ." He
stopped. "I cannot speak what I would say, but you understand? Yes?" Lee looked up at the tall GI, trying to stifle the
tears that welled up in his eyes.

"Yes. Yes, I understand," Bill said softly. He paused. "Come
on," he said brusquely. "Let's go back to the barracks and I
will show you where we will be."

That night they went over the instructions again. Bill had
a large map of Korea spread out on the bunk, and he had

traced the road in heavy black pencil. To where it branched off just beyond Uijongbu.

"You will have to wait about two weeks after I go. By that time I will have gotten your equipment from the supply room if I can, and I will have made some arrangements for your food. Now, you remember how you can tell where the place is?"

"Yes," Lee nodded. "I will know it by the big rock on the top of the hill. It looks as though the rock were going to fall. You will be in the valley behind that hill."

"Yes. You can tell that you are right, because you will see the antenna masts that we will put up on that hill. You can't miss it. I wish that I could get you a sleeping bag. But they are already short in supply. Without one, you will be cold."

"I don't care. It will not matter."

Within a few hours that gray morning came when Lee stood on the main street of the compound, his hands deep in his pockets shrugging against the icy wind that swept over him. Bill made some last-minute checks on the radio equipment, made sure that the power unit was securely fastened to the radio van, and then with a wave to Lee, he jumped up into the cab of the truck, and shifted the gears. The heavy green van rolled slowly down the bumpy road, paused at the gate, and disappeared into the city. Lee turned back to the barracks. It would be time to get the water for the others, and to get the new can of oil for the stoves. He forced himself to follow his routine methodically. It helped a little to still the ache that split his throat.

The routine carried him through those next two weeks, and he tried not to think ahead or back to the past. Just think of now, the job to be done now, and the time will go that much faster, he thought.

At work this was not too hard to do. But at home, when the bare monotony of his life settled in upon him, he had a hard time. Too many thoughts from the past flashed like summer lightning across his lonely mind.

His mother did not speak too often to him. She kept hoping against hope that he would change his mind, and not go. She devoted more and more time to the baby, leaving Lee alone with his thoughts.

Lee could see that she was not happy. They had all been together for such a short time, and now he was leaving again. They could not speak now. That silent communication that had been there before was gone. They were separated by worlds of experience. There was no bridge, the distance between them was too great. But he was her son, and in his heart he reached out for her like a lost child, and she reached for him, but, somehow, they never touched. And all the rest was quiet.

The night before he was to leave, Lee sat in the kitchen by the fire. His mother was beside him looking away into space. After a long while, she came back to the present.

"Then you are going north tomorrow?" She stood up smoothing her full skirts, not looking at him.

"Yes. The two weeks have passed. I will keep my promise."

"Why?" Choo's voice was loud in the small room. "Why must you follow them? You have been close enough to fighting. You have seen enough war." She stopped to control herself. "Maybe this time you will die. Do you want that?" She began taking live coals out of the fire and putting them into a wide brass bowl to take to her room for warmth.

"Live, die, I do not think of that. This man has been good to me, and to you, too. He has given us much. Now, in the North, he will need help. I can help him."

"There are other ways. You do not have to go there to show your loyalty." She tried to think of some other way that he could help. There was none. She felt impatience that her son should feel so deeply concerned for a foreigner. If it had been his brother . . .

Lee wanted to say so much more. He looked at the tired woman that was his mother and thought, *"Oh, Mother, what can I say to you that you will understand? A new world has been born in Korea. The old is dead. You do not know this. To you we are a country at war. You think that the war will pass, and then everything will be as it was. You think that Korea is unchanged . . . that the plum tree will bloom again in the spring and all will be as you remember. What words can I speak that will help you to understand? My heart is so full . . . the unspoken word bursts within me like a seed in spring soil . . . but I cannot say what I would . . ."*

He looked at her as she set out the dishes for tomorrow's breakfast. "It is a long way. I will leave early so that I can go far the first day." Lee spoke gently, firmly. He was the head of the house. His mother had to obey.

"Yes, I will wake you early." She scattered salt over the open charcoal bowl to cut the smoke. "I have made rice cakes to stop the hunger," she said, turning away from him. Her face was without expression, but there were tears in her thoughts: *". . . Do not go, my son . . . You will be cold and alone. I can feel it in my woman's heart. Do not leave . . . if you leave, my house will be as empty as my heart . . . stay . . . stay . . ."*

She did not speak her thoughts. Stooping, she picked up

the bowl. "You sleep, now." She went out of the kitchen quickly. After a moment, Lee went to his own room.

As he lay in the darkness, sleep would not come. Lee heard the wind rising outside and thought, "It will be cold tomorrow . . . such a long walk." There was much fighting there now, the men in the company had said. He turned restlessly, but it was very late before a heavy sleep crushed his mind.

He awoke a short time later. His mother was standing just inside the door calling to him softly. She held a candle high in her hand. It was time to get up. He heard her go to the kitchen, and as he dressed the rattling sounds of the morning came to him.

He ate his breakfast quickly, not feeling hungry, just very cold. When he had finished, he went to his brother's room, and shook him awake.

"I am getting ready to leave now. I wanted to say good-by," he whispered as the younger boy rubbed the sleep out of his eyes.

"I will get up . . ."

"No." Lee interrupted Yung Sin. "No. I think that it will be easier for Mother if you do not." Then in quick words he repeated the things his father had said to him that night so long ago. "And if anything does happen . . . I mean, if

I do not come back for a while, remember that you are in charge. Do your job well."

"I will," Yung Sin promised.

"Now I go. You sleep." Quickly Lee went out the door. He stopped in his room to get his dictionaries, and one book on the life of Lincoln that Bill had given him, and then he went to the kitchen.

Choo stood by the door. The baby was asleep in her arms. Lee looked down at the child for a long moment, and then he said, "I must go now." Choo nodded silently. Lee looked at her, and she smiled at him saying, "Be safe, my son."

He nodded and touching her hand for a second, he went quickly out of the door.

Lee looked back at the city from the top of the long hill. He could see the jagged ruins against the dawn sky like accusing fingers. A great sadness filled him as he looked down on the remains of the once beautiful capital. There was so little left. He turned his back and walked steadily north.

The wind was cold and savage as it whipped south through the icy mountains, over the frozen valleys toward Seoul. In the thick flint-colored clouds overhead was the grim promise of snow. He bent his head against the cold, and plodded on.

There was the usual trickle of refugees filing south, even at this early hour. Sometimes Lee would stop for a moment and ask what the news of fighting was. Many did not know, but from those who had heard, he found out that things were about the same as a few days ago. The UN was losing ground here, gaining ground there. Many guerrilla bands swept down from the north attacking, pillaging. They were hard to catch, as they posed as farmers in the day and attacked small stations at night, destroying all that they could not carry away.

These tales disturbed Lee, and he walked faster pushing the miles behind him as fast as possible. He did not stop to talk with the other refugees on the road, as he was jealous of the time that they took from his walking.

The freezing cold, and the endless walking were exhausting him very quickly. But still his mind was alert to danger. When he saw a military check-point ahead he would cut off through the frosty rice paddies, and go far around the station. This made his walk much longer, but he knew that if he were careful, he would not be caught and sent back.

Sometimes he would get a ride from an army truck or jeep. Tears would almost come as he would sit in the jouncing vehicle, out of the icy wind for a little while, watching the miles roll past. He found the drivers that picked him up very friendly, and he learned much about the fighting. But there was no word about radio communications. The drivers were always from some other division, engineers or medical, and they had no knowledge of communications.

The first day, he had come easily halfway. As it was getting dark, he had to find a place to stay. If he were on the road at night, he would be arrested. The police patrols permitted no travel after dark.

He went from farmhouse to farmhouse looking for shelter. He finally found a farmer who would take him in. After showing him the room where Lee could sleep, the farmer retired leaving Lee alone with a man who had also been taken in. The refugee was a very old man, and from his dress Lee could see that he was a scholar. Lee bowed to the man, not speaking. He knew that one never spoke to a scholar until spoken to. The refugee's eyes gleamed hungrily as he saw Lee unwrap the last of the rice cakes.

"You are going north?" the old man asked, still watching the food.

"Yes, sir," Lee answered. He saw the man's look, and laid one of the cakes before him.

"There is much fighting up there. Last night many soldiers died. Many." He ate rapidly, plucking every fallen crumb from the mat with his talon-like fingers.

"Where do they fight, sir?"

"In the west. Many Chinese came in the night." The scholar looked greedily at the remaining rice cake. Lee gave it to him, asking, "Did you hear anything of radio communications?" He asked the question desperately, knowing that this man could tell him nothing.

"Of those I did not hear. Ah, it is a bad thing. It is a very bad thing that has happened to Korea." He licked the oil from his fingers. "I think that the enemy will come again to Seoul. They fight like ten thousand devils. I am going to go all the way to Pusan. And if they come to Seoul, I will go to Japan. I wish to spend my last days in peace."

"But we have the strength of the world with us now. They will not come back to Seoul." Lee spoke quickly, forgetting that one never disagreed with a scholar.

"A child's answer," the man answered coldly. He lay back not wanting to speak further.

Lee huddled in his corner sleepless and cold. If only he could go faster. If only he did not have to waste the night like this. The animal of fear was in him, too, biting at his heart with sharp pointed teeth. At the first sign of dawn, he left without waiting to thank the farmer.

There was much more traffic on the road today, but no one stopped to pick him up. The men driving the trucks were dirty and unshaven. Occasionally an ambulance would speed past, its horn blasting a path around the heavy army trucks. Lee walked quickly, ignoring his empty stomach that growled with hunger, his feet that were numb with cold. In the distance he could see the snow-covered hills. Only one thought pounded again and again against his exhausted brain.

"I must not stop . . . I must not stop . . . I promised . . ." He fastened his eyes on the distant hills, and forced his legs to keep on walking.

"I must not stop . . ." he repeated the words like a chant, again and again in his mind, aloud. Just beyond those frigid hills there was warmth, food. He would be all right as soon as he got there. He could see Bill's face before him, and a smile cracked its way across his frozen lips.

At noon it began to snow. The hills were very close. Lee pushed on, almost falling with the aching tiredness that filled him. His boots soon became wet from the snow. There was almost no feeling left in his legs. He forced himself to go on.

In the afternoon a snub-nosed British lorry stopped and the driver offered him a ride. Lee pulled himself up into the seat, brushing the snow from his face. He tried to smile at the driver, but the muscles just wouldn't work.

"Why, you poor little tyke, you must be near frozen," the driver said loudly. He groped beneath the seat, and brought out a huge thermos jug. "Here, this tea is what you need. Nice and hot." He handed the bottle to Lee, and slowed the truck so that the hot liquid would not spill while Lee's numbed hands poured it into the metal cup. "Drink as much as you want."

The hot tea began to bring his body back to life. After a few swallows he asked the driver what had happened to make so much traffic.

"Oh, they had a little rumpus up on Bunker Hill last night. The reds blasted the Marines off the hill, and a lot were hurt. Won't last long, though. Those Americans will probably have it back before many days pass."

Lee tried to fight the waves of exhaustion that rose up in him from the warmth of the engine, and the tea.

"What part are you headed for, lad?" Lee described the area, and was delighted when the man said, "Oh, yes. I know where that is. I turn off about two miles before we reach it. You shouldn't have any trouble finding it after I drop you off."

Just two miles to go after he got off . . . just two miles . . .

The tea helped Lee. He felt much better when he climbed down from the truck a few miles later. He smiled up into the ruddy face of the driver as he thanked him and said good-by. He watched the truck roll away at the fork in the road, and then he began walking down the left branch. The road curved deep into the hills, and far ahead Lee could see it winding ribbon-like into the snow. On his left, the edge of the road dropped sharply into a deep valley far below. In the center of the valley, a frozen river wound its way, and Lee could see what had once been a railway bridge spanning the water. It was now a twisted, rusting mass of metal and concrete, with a few freight cars overturned nearby.

The snow fell more heavily as he walked, and through it he could hear the ever-present sound of guns.

It was late in the afternoon when Lee saw the rock on the edge of the hill. He could barely make it out through the snow. Hurrying forward, he left the road, and began to climb the hill. He strained his eyes through the white curtain, until he saw what he was seeking. The tall antenna mast rose slim and dark against the sky seeming to touch the cloud mass above. Halfway up the hill, his heart gave a leap of happiness as he made out the other mast farther away on the hilltop. Lee hurried upward with a great joy in him. So near, so near . . . just a few more steps.

Higher . . . his frozen boots slipped in the snow, and he had trouble making his stiff legs carry him up over the rutted hill. Behind him, to the west, he could hear the frenzied sound of gunfire, much closer now. The articulate chatter of machine guns stood out from the boom-boom of the heavy artillery. He had to stop to catch his breath. He hunched down, squatting in the snow for a moment, then he renewed his climb, his breath coming in short jagged gasps.

And, with a supreme effort, he clawed his way to the top of the hill, and slowly stood straight.

He wiped the snow from his eyes, and looked up. A chill of terror sparked through him rooting him to the spot. Before him, the antenna wire was dangling, slapping against the dark mast. He walked over to it, not understanding, and held the end in his fingers. Cut . . . It dropped out of his fingers, and the wind caught it. He went to the edge of the hill and looked down into the valley. A great cry tore from his throat as he saw the burned radio van, and the dark frosted rectangle where the tent had been.

Lee sprawled, and fell down the hill. Words, Korean and English, formed soundlessly on his lips. His breath came in short whimpering gasps. He saw a few dead Communist soldiers sprawled in the snow.

Reaching the valley floor, he ran to the radio truck, and forced himself to look at the four bodies that were inside. He did not see Bill. Jumping down from the charred van, he saw a mound in the snow near where the tent had been. He ran to it, brushing the snow from its face. No, no it was not he.

There was another body in the snow . . . No, that one was too short.

Six. Where was the seventh? Had one escaped? Where was . . .

Then he saw.

A little way up the hill a grotesque shape was hanging over a boulder. Lee went slowly up to it. An Ml rifle was on the ground nearby . . . Lee knelt down and raised the dead man's head.

Yes.

He straightened the corpse's twisted limbs, and he closed the staring eyes. Holding Bill's head in his lap, he leaned back listening to the distant guns. They were muffled now by the surrounding hills. He looked up to the far mountains that rose soft through the falling snow behind the white hills. He could see the naked, sharp-branched trees, their limbs dead and dark against the white world. The valley was so very beautiful. The snow had begun to cover him, the large flakes making a protective cover. He drank in the harsh beauty of the valley and the hills.

Then he closed his eyes, waiting . . .

Epilogue

AT SEOUL AIRPORT a plane is ready for take-off. A large group of well-wishers cry their good-bys to a young man who hurries onto the field toward the waiting craft. His name is checked, and he climbs the steps. Turning, he waves to the shouting people crowding at the gate. His mother is there. She holds a small boy of four high, so that he, too, can see. Beside her, another boy stands solemn-faced, and waves.

Within minutes, the plane taxis onto the airstrip, is cleared, and begins its run. The sunlight glints off the rising wings as it banks and turns away from Seoul, toward the Sea of Japan.

This is the first lap of a long trip to the United States. The young man is going to America to live with his new father, a former soldier who found him at the front. In only a few months he will be adopted, taking his new father's name. In a few months, he will be at school learning to be an artist, eventually illustrating the book that is based on his life during the war.

For this is a fictional account of his years during the early part of the Korean War. Much of this story actually happened to him; some happened to the people he knew. All of it was important to him as a Korean boy involved in one of the tragic wars of our time.

R. W. C.